What had she been thinking, chasing after Dr. Dangerous like that?

The man was probably nuts. He was most certainly eccentric and showed signs of agoraphobia. Yet she'd cornered him, argued— she'd touched him. All mistakes when it came to self-preservation. He was so far out of her league—professionally, socially, economically, intellectually—that it was laughable to think she'd had the nerve to confront him.

But it was the man who had her all mixed up inside, not the name.

Her reactions to him had been varied, unexpected, overpowering. There'd been an initial rush of sexual awareness that left her feverish. He was so tall, so hardened, so male. Trading words with him made the blood hum through her veins. He was such a complexity of words and actions and mysterious motivations that she was driven to puzzle him out.

And then she'd seen his face and touched his hand and felt…pity.

JULIE MILLER

BEAST IN THE TOWER

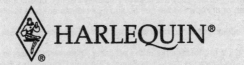

HARLEQUIN®

TORONTO • NEW YORK • LONDON
AMSTERDAM • PARIS • SYDNEY • HAMBURG
STOCKHOLM • ATHENS • TOKYO • MILAN • MADRID
PRAGUE • WARSAW • BUDAPEST • AUCKLAND

For Dr. Todd Pankratz and his staff.

Plus, to the surgical staff, admission specialists and 3rd floor nurses at Mary Lanning Memorial Hospital in Hastings, Nebraska:

I owe you more than words can say here.
I feel better.
Thanks.

ISBN-13: 978-0-373-88740-8
ISBN-10: 0-373-88740-X

BEAST IN THE TOWER

ABOUT THE AUTHOR

Julie Miller attributes her passion for writing romance to all those fairy tales she read growing up, and to shyness. Encouragement from her family to write down all those feelings she couldn't express became a love for the written word. She gets continued support from her fellow members of the Prairieland Romance Writers, where she serves as the resident grammar goddess. This award-winning author and teacher has published several paranormal romances. Inspired by the likes of Agatha Christie and Encyclopedia Brown, Julie believes the only thing better than a good mystery is a good romance.

Born and raised in Missouri, she now lives in Nebraska with her husband, son and smiling guard dog, Maxie. Write to Julie at P.O. Box 5162, Grand Island, NE 68802-5162.

Books by Julie Miller

HARLEQUIN INTRIGUE

699—THE ROOKIE†
719—KANSAS CITY'S BRAVEST†
748—UNSANCTIONED MEMORIES†
779—LAST MAN STANDING†
819—PARTNER-PROTECTOR*
841—POLICE BUSINESS*
880—FORBIDDEN CAPTOR
898—SEARCH AND SEIZURE*
947—BABY JANE DOE*
966—BEAST IN THE TOWER

†The Taylor Clan
*The Precinct

CAST OF CHARACTERS

Dr. Damon Sinclair—Brilliant researcher or mad scientist? Rumors have surrounded the reclusive billionaire since tragedy disfigured him and drove his wife to suicide.

Kit Snow—She abandoned her dreams when her parents mysteriously died. Now she's come home to reopen their downtown diner and take care of her makeshift family.

Matthew Snow—Kit's brother is dealing with the changes in his life by making some bad choices.

Helen Hodges—More than a housekeeper. She loves the gifted boy she raised as though he were her own flesh and blood, and the feeling's mutual.

Easting Davitz—Damon's executive liaison and link to the outside world.

Ken Kenichi—A foreign businessman who'd like to acquire Sinclair Labs and all its patents.

Germane Knight—He holds the secret recipe for Snow's Barbecue Sauce. What other secrets does he possess?

J. T. Kronemeyer—The current construction foreman on the Sinclair Tower.

Miranda Sinclair—Her death haunts the husband she left behind.

The Sinclair Tower—Madman's folly or work of art? Rising above the Kansas City skyline, this architectural wonder hides many secrets. And a few dead bodies.

Prologue

The dust settling from the tired old walls coated the warped, three-legged chair like a layer of gray velvet, undisturbed by the passage of time. Since it offered the only place to sit in this abandoned room, standing was the preferred option.

The room had made some banker's assistant a nice, cozy office back in the building's heyday. Now it was a decrepit eyesore, marred by peeling plaster and exposed studs in the crumbling walls, good for nothing more than meetings like this one.

Just another example of misused funds and misguided dreams. Dr. Damon Sinclair had been a sentimental fool to purchase this thirty-story high-rise and hire architects and historians to research its history so he could restore it to all its glory. He was an even bigger fool for trusting the wrong people.

But one man's disadvantage was another—
"I've got them."

Ah, yes, the hired help had arrived. A few minutes late, but carrying something that could make his tardiness forgivable. Anticipation cleared the sinuses and made the eyes sharply perceptive. "Let me see them."

Electricity hadn't run on this floor of the newly renamed Sinclair Tower for years, but the heavy flashlight provided all the illumination necessary to inspect the treasure the short, stocky workman handed over. He was breathing hard from the exertion of the past hour or so, and the grime hiding beneath his fingernails was as distasteful as the room surrounding them.

But a normal aversion to filthy things was momentarily forgotten as the culmination of so much planning was about to come to fruition. Retribution was only a fortunate by-product of the millions waiting to be made. Patience had allowed the plan to go forward, but tonight it was asking too much to wait for the privacy of a cleaner place before opening the leather-bound books.

The three binders were heavy with the weight of possibilities. Thumbing through the pages of scribbled notes and computer read-outs was like following a map to the pot of gold at the end of the rainbow.

Only, the little leprechaun sent to retrieve the map had forgotten one very important item.

Inhale deeply, exhale slowly. Patience. Patience.

"You've already rigged the explosion?"

The sweaty man hired for his alleged expertise nodded. "Yeah. The unstable base and volatile acid will *accidentally* meet in—" he paused to check his watch before raising a cocky grin "—fifteen minutes and twenty-two seconds. No one will be able to trace what we've done, or even that we've been there."

"We?"

The incompetent fool had the audacity to laugh. "Yeah, right, I know. You were never even here in the building."

"That's not the only mistake you've made, you idiot." The binders dropped like a gauntlet between them, sending up a billowing cloud of dust.

The little leprechaun frowned, perplexed by the displeasure. "What's wrong? Shouldn't we be leaving?"

Sheer willpower stifled the urge to sneeze. "Where are the codes? The difference between these binders—and binders with the codes—is ten million dollars. These formulas will take years to decipher without them."

"I looked where you said. I looked everywhere I could think of. Your information was wrong. The codes weren't in his lab." He backed toward the door frame and glanced into the hallway, as if expecting to be discovered. Had the idiot been followed? Maybe he'd been stupid enough to use the freight elevator, the noise of which would certainly alert those do-gooders who ran the restaurant on the ground floor that there were trespassers on the upper floors of the building.

"You took the stairs, didn't you? I warned you to use the stairs."

The words fell on deaf ears. "Look, the blast won't affect us down here, but the cops'll question anybody on the premises. Those fifteen minutes will go by faster than you think. We need to get out of here."

Inhale. Exhale.

"It will take months—maybe years—of research to recreate Dr. Sinclair's formulas from these notes. My investors may not be as patient as I—"

The little man dared to point a finger. "I brought you the files you specified, replaced them with the fakes so no one would know they were stolen, just like you said. And hell, yeah, I took the stairs."

"I told you we'd need the codes."

"They weren't there! I turned that place inside out. They must be hidden someplace else. I don't know where else to look, what else to do."

"Yes, your incompetence is staggering." The gun slipped from its waistband holster as easily as the decision to use it was made. Damon Sinclair was a crafty bastard, but he could be beaten. Though not if there was someone on the team who couldn't get the job done. "It's cost me more than I anticipated already."

His gaze narrowed and focused on the gun. "What are you gonna do?"

Aim between the eyes. Pull the trigger before you can run. The leprechaun's head jerked back. He hit the wall and slumped to the floor. Dead. "Get better help."

Chapter One

The Present

"My wife will be worried if I'm late getting home. I've been out of town on business this week."

"Take him straight to the shelter." Hiding her sad smile, Katherine Snow wrapped a ten-dollar bill around the disposable cup of coffee and passed it through the open window to the taxi driver on the late-night shift. She shivered, missing the warmth of the cup the instant it left her hands. "I owe you one, Tariq."

But the cabbie shook his head and tried to return the cash. "If this is your good coffee, it is payment enough."

Kit pulled her fingers inside the sleeves of her sweater and tucked them against her chest. "You know I always brew a fresh pot for night owls like us."

"The shelter is just a couple of blocks away."

He pushed the ten-dollar bill her way again. "Save this for Matty's college fund. You should make Old Henry walk."

One, she had no clue whether or not her teenage brother would make it through his last semester of high school, much less go on to college; two, even with her limited profit margin she could spare ten dollars; and three, "Old Henry," as Tariq had dubbed him, was in no shape to walk anywhere. Especially since he thought "home" included a wife who had passed away a decade ago.

Henry would never find his way through the minefield of construction equipment that lined the streets and surrounded the Sinclair Building where her diner was located. "Two weeks ago, one of Kronemeyer's electricians touched a live wire upstairs and had a heart attack. And what about that old concrete cornice that fell off the side of the building? If Henry hadn't come inside to get out of the cold, he would have had his brains bashed in. Or the masonry worker who supposedly just walked off the job—without collecting his pay-check or telling his boss to shove it—and hasn't been seen since? Believe me, I'm happy to pay for Henry's cab," Kit insisted.

Henry Phipps had come in for a free meal of leftovers and coffee to sober him up enough to allow him admission to the area shelter. And just like the other nights when he'd shown up at closing, Kit had refused to turn him away.

Tariq shook his head and argued, "You do too much."

"I try to tell her the same thing. She doesn't listen."

Kit rolled her eyes up at the pepper-haired black man who'd helped her load their last customer into the cab's backseat. "You're not saying I'm pigheaded, are you, Germane?"

"I'm saying that once you set your mind to a thing…ah, hell." He shrugged and surrendered to the inevitable. "You're just like your daddy was."

"A great cook?"

Germane snorted. "A sucker for every sad story that came through his front door. I wish you had more of your mama's good sense. And who does most of the cookin' around here?"

Kit grinned and linked one arm through his, bowing to the master short-order cook. Germane Knight had been a family friend for far too long to take any of his grousing seriously. Though they'd served together as combat medics in Vietnam, he was as big a softie as her father had been. "Fine. You run the kitchen, I run everything else. Like customer relations. It's after midnight, below freezing and it's snowing again. Good sense says it isn't safe for anyone to be outside on his own."

"I am giving in even if you are not, G." Tariq raised his cup in a toast to Kit, then tossed the ten-dollar bill to a confused Henry in the backseat. "We will all freeze to death if we sit here and argue until she changes her mind."

"Don't I know it." Germane had a surprisingly deep belly laugh for such a tall, slender man. He dodged Kit's elbow to his ribs, reached out and thumped the roof of the cab, clearing Tariq to be on his way. "Be safe, my friend."

With a wave, Tariq checked the light traffic, then whipped away from the curb in a U-turn to avoid construction in the lane ahead. Kit and Germane jumped back as sooty slush spun from beneath the tires up onto the sidewalk. Kit was still shaking the glop off her boots when Germane pulled her back toward the brightly lit windows of the Snow Family Barbecue Grill and Diner.

"C'mon, girl. We'd best get out of the cold air ourselves and get this place shut down for the night. I'm feelin' the chill in my knees somethin' fierce."

"In a minute." Giving his arm a reassuring pat, Kit pushed Germane toward the diner's front door. "The dishes are already in the washer. Go ahead and turn off the neon signs and start cleaning the grill. I'll be there in a sec to take care of the pans and count down the money."

Kit huddled inside her cable-knit sweater and

peered into the filmy shadows beyond the circles of lamplight dotting the street to the north and south. An older woman slowed her car and pulled into the parking garage next door. A pair of faceless figures buried their faces in their hoods and collars as they left the shelter of Hannity's Bar and cut across the slickening street.

Could the young man in the red-and-gold Kansas City Chiefs parka be Matt? He wasn't old enough to buy a drink, but that kid was rebelling with a vengeance against the forced parenting of his older sister. Kit had left graduate school and come home after their parents' unexpected deaths, thinking he needed her. She knew she needed him. But they were each dealing with their grief in different ways. She thought Matt wanted a home, but apparently, her one-time Stanford-bound brother just wanted his space.

But a Chiefs parka was common enough this time of year in a football-crazed city like K.C. When the two bar patrons turned north away from the diner, Kit wondered anew where Matt could be at 12:00 a.m. on a Thursday night. She was going to have to do the tough-love thing and ground his tardy ass for being out so late on a school night.

Shivering at the pending sense of loss she couldn't quite explain, Kit looked up and down the street one more time. She couldn't see much else through the steel scaffolding and plastic sheeting that framed the building's facade and curved into the side alley. Though the work on her own first-floor apartment and business had been completed three months ago, the construction team renovating the twenty-nine floors above her in the Depression-era Sinclair Building never seemed to run out of projects.

The workers were the diner's best customers for lunch. But, along with the handful of tenants on the second and third floors who'd stuck it out through first one construction company, then another, she suspected she wasn't the only one tired of her absent landlord's penchant for historic perfection. Heavy equipment had blocked the sidewalk and torn up the street for more than a year now, turning three lanes of traffic into two, and giving petty thieves, gang-bangers and the homeless plenty of places to hide at night. She suspected some unwanted squatters had even found their way into a few of the unfinished apartments above her.

Though she could admire the unseen Sinclair heir for trying to make this block of downtown Kansas City the same tourist-and-young-professional draw that Wesport or the Plaza to the south were, Kit feared that the working-class locals would be forced to move before any new influx of business could save them.

Kit's parents hadn't owned any pharmaceutical empires like the Sinclairs did. They couldn't pack up and go to a second home in the islands when the weather turned bitter and the construction got in the way. They'd toughed it out and had paid the ultimate price in the fire that had taken everything. This block of Kansas City had been their home. True, Kit had gone off to college to pursue her science degrees, and had dreamed of working in a criminology lab in New York City or Chicago. But she'd returned when she was needed. To find out why her parents had died. To rebuild their diner and maintain their dream.

This was her home now. And her brother's. Along with the countless castoffs from society like Germane and the handful of loyal workers she employed. They all needed her to succeed. She didn't have time to want or dream.

Kit tilted her face and squinted up into the falling snow. The ominous shadows of the Sinclair Building's Art Deco carvings and dark rows of high-tech replacement windows towered above her. The far-removed penthouse apartments on the top floors were completely swallowed up by the raw night sky. If the construction delays didn't end, and the troubling rise in neighborhood crime didn't—

"Watchin' isn't gonna make that boy come home any sooner." Germane's sympathetic warning stirred Kit from her thoughts. "This is the second night this week Matty's missed his curfew."

At eighteen, six years her junior, Kit's brother looked more man than boy. And legally, she supposed she didn't have any right to set boundaries and expectations for him. But even if he wouldn't accept her hugs, she intended to protect him. From gangs, drinking, crime—from himself. He could hate her guts if he wanted, but Matthew Snow Jr. was going to make it to adulthood and make something of himself. She'd sworn that promise at her parents' graves.

She couldn't quite raise a smile. "You noticed, huh?"

"He's giving you worry lines beside those pretty gray eyes."

"He'll be here." She hoped. The worry that was never far from her thoughts cut through her like the bite of the winter wind. *Doing* had become a lot easier than *feeling* lately. That was how *she* dealt with the loss. She pushed Germane through the diner's front door and locked it behind her. She'd wait until Matt showed up before pulling down the cage that shielded the front windows. "C'mon. We've got work to do."

TEN MINUTES LATER Kit jumped at the scream from the alley. Elbow-deep in hot, sudsy water, she chilled at the words she heard through the kitchen's back door.

"You?"

"Shut up and let go, you hag!"

"Take it. Please, just take—"

She preferred screams to the muffled thud and sudden, eerie silence.

"Germane!" He was mopping out by the tables. But she was just a few feet away from the shouts and scuffle in the alley. Kit tightened her grip around the iron skillet she'd been washing and ran to the exit. "Call 911!"

"Kit! Don't you—"

But she was already out the door at the top of the loading dock. *Not Matt. Please don't let it be Matt.* The crunching of snow drew her attention to the steel scaffolding beyond the light over her back door. She spotted the groceries scattered across the ground and hurried down the concrete steps toward the torn sack they belonged to.

"Next time, old lady, you'll shut up when I tell you to."

Kit's eyes adjusted to the sight of two young men in saggy jeans and hooded parkas—one bearing the distinctive arrowhead of the Chiefs—squatting beside a woman's still form in the slush near the garbage cans. "Matty?"

The bigger of the two stopped digging through the woman's purse and swung around. Black hair and little else was visible above the scarf he'd tied over his face. *Not Matt.*

Blood boiled in Kit's veins, overriding both relief and fear. "Get away from her. Get away!"

Kit charged before the startled man could rise. She smacked him in the shoulder, sending both purse and attacker flying. Unfazed by his fluent foreign curses, she jumped over the woman's skinned-up legs and raised the skillet to go after the smaller man.

But a third pair of arms grabbed her from behind and slung her against the building. The skillet banged against the wall, stinging her fingers and popping her grip. It clattered to the ground as the man she'd struck lurched forward, wanting his own retribution. "Nobody hits me, bitch!"

He shoved her before she had a chance to react. She smacked into solid limestone. The air whooshed from her lungs and her head spun from the dizzying contact.

"Get out of here! Now!" Blurry hands pulled the man in the Chiefs parka back and urged him to run.

Kit sank to her knees as the three men scattered. By the time she could fill her lungs with cold air and clear her head, they were gone. Along with the woman's purse.

Kit didn't waste time pursuing them. The older

woman, groaning but not moving, was a greater concern. Kit crawled over and knelt beside her, quickly assessing that her unfocused eyes were open and her pulse was beating. Recognizing the snowy cap of hair and slight build beneath the thick wool coat and knitted scarf, she asked, "Helen?"

Recognize was a generous term. The woman came into the diner for an occasional cup of tea, but usually just nodded and smiled when they passed each other on the sidewalk or in the parking garage. She seemed friendly enough, but very private. She'd probably been a resident around here for years, and was being cautious about the alarming changes in her environment.

Any wonder? The dangerous proof was the fresh tracks in the snow, exiting the alley between the parking garage and the Sinclair Building's side entrances.

"Helen? That's your name, right?" The woman gasped as Kit peeled the wool scarf away from the bloody wound at her temple. She'd had enough training in her forensic classes to identify the long, round indentation of the wound. Those greedy bastards had hit this fly-weight woman with a pipe, or maybe shoved her into one of the scaffolding bars. But this wasn't the time for Kit's innate curiosity to kick in. The woman was going into shock.

"Germane!"

Where was he?

Kit didn't want to leave the woman's side. Briefly peeling off her sweater and baring her flanks and back to the chapping cold, Kit removed her cotton turtleneck and pressed it against Helen's wound while she redressed. "Where do you live? What's your last name?"

Though she moaned at the contact, Helen was fading.

"Hang on." She shouted over her shoulder, "Germane!"

"Right behind you, girl." Germane limped through the back door, carrying a blanket beneath his arm and a cell phone against his ear. He relayed information to the dispatcher as he hurried down the stairs. "That's right. The Sinclair Building at Ninth and Walnut. Looks like an elderly woman in the alley on the north side." He paused and frowned. "I didn't see nothin'. But if you don't get that ambulance here soon, the cops'll be investigating a murder, not a mugging."

"Germane?" Kit took the blanket from him as he shut his phone and braced a hand on her shoulder to kneel on the opposite side of the woman. Kit winced at the bruise that must already be swelling on her shoulder blade.

His sharp eyes didn't miss a trick. "How bad are *you* hurt?"

"I had a run-in with the wall, but it's nothing serious." Kit skipped the details and unfolded the blanket to tuck it around Helen's slight figure. Germane was already listening to the older woman's breathing and checking for pupil response. "How is she?"

"She's got a concussion for sure. Hell, they could've cracked her skull, as deep as that wound goes."

Kit turned toward the end of the alley where the footprints disappeared. "The muggers took her purse, and she hasn't given me her name. I think it's Helen, but I don't know who to contact or what to tell the paramedics. Do you know her?"

"Keep talking to her," Germane advised, measuring the woman's pulse. "All I know is, she lives upstairs. She's been in a few times, pesterin' me for my barbecue sauce recipe. Says she used to make as good. She's always by herself, though, so maybe there isn't anybody to cook for anymore."

Or anyone to call. Kit smoothed away the droplets of melting snow from the woman's cool cheek. "Helen? Can you hear me? Look at me, Helen."

The rheumy blue eyes blinked. Her pale lips slurred a question. "Are you dead?"

"What?" Kit panicked when Helen's eyes drifted shut. "No. I'm very much alive. And so are you. Stay with me, Helen." She pulled the woman's bony hand between her own and tried to rub some warmth back into it. "Helen? You're not alone. Stay with me."

Her cold hand went limp in Kit's grasp as she murmured, "We're all dead."

Chapter Two

The fire was all around him, climbing up the walls and leaping across the ceiling.

Dr. Damon Sinclair crawled toward the emergency exit at the back of his lab. The door where he'd entered minutes earlier to pick up his notes for tomorrow's board meeting was no longer an escape route. The glass entryway had shattered and the fire was now licking its way into the hallway on the opposite side.

Beakers exploded from the heat and rained glass on his back. Their contents fed the flames. The few sprinklers that had survived the explosion were doing little more than creating steam as they spat out water at irregular intervals.

If he hadn't smelled the chemicals—if he hadn't reacted to the searing stench of the volatile combination and dived beneath his desk to avoid the initial blast—he'd already be dead. The milliseconds of warning had left him with a head wound, an armful of research documentation and a chance at survival. But that chance was slim if he couldn't find a way out.

Blinded by the blood seeping into his left eye, feverish from the blazing heat, he moved forward by instinct alone. When he hit a wall instead of the exit, he knew he had to make a choice. He set the binders on the floor with a reverence for the miracles contained inside. His work could save lives—it had saved lives. And now he'd set it aside to save his own life.

The answers were all inside his head, anyway. Given enough time, he could recreate them if he had to. If he ever got out of this hellfire, he'd have all the time in the world to...

A farewell look at his work elicited a choice curse.

"What the hell is this garbage?" These weren't his notes. Just pages and pages of numbers and equations that didn't make sense. He hurled the worthless counterfeits into the growing flames.

Was that what this was about? This treacherous, purposeful destruction, just to hide a theft?

Whoever was responsible... Whoever had planted that damned incendiary... Reams of notes and calculations—gone. Successful equations and rejected experiments he could learn from—gone. State-of-the-art technology designed by his own hands...

His hands…

"Son of a bitch!"

They were on fire.

Damon reengaged his brain and fought off the groggy disorientation that consumed him.

Whoever was responsible for this betrayal would not go unpunished. There were means a man of his intellect and bank account could use to make the bastard who'd sabotaged his life's work pay.

He let the rage suffuse him. Give him strength. He clutched his arms to his stomach and doubled over to stifle the flames with his own body. "You'll pay." The heat from his own hands seared his flesh. "You'll pay."

"Help! Damon! Help me!"

"Miranda?" A pain far more cruel than any physical torture twisted in the pit of his stomach. Oh, no. God, no. "Miranda!"

His wife's screams hurt worse than the scorching agony of the skin blistering on his fingers. Her terror cut deeper than the shrapnel in his forehead. He'd gladly give up any medical secret he could devise, but please, please, spare his wife.

"Miranda!" He shouldered aside burning tables, melting plastic and shattered glass, desperately searching through the roiling smoke. "Miranda! Ans—" He choked on the toxic gases coating his lungs and crumpled to the floor. A hoarse cough racked his body and ravaged his throat before he could summon the strength to push to his knees. "Answer me!"

"Damon!"

Her screech of desperation drove him on. He crawled through corrosive puddles and ruined work and unknown treachery to find the only thing that truly mattered. "Miranda? Please. Keep talking. I'll find—" Coughing cut like broken glass through his raw throat. The spasms drained his strength and he collapsed again. But he pulled himself toward her ragged sobs. "I'm coming." His administrative assistant. His love. His life. Work be damned. "I'm coming."

"Damon…"

A chunk of ceiling gave way and crashed to the floor, shooting up a snarling roar of white heat and orange flame. Damon rolled to the side, sucking in the last breath of oxygen hovering above the floor. The firefighters and paramedics were on their way. But even if they were already in the building, they had twenty-eight stories to climb. Damon was his wife's last—her only—hope for survival.

"Miranda!"

He found her curled into a ball in the corner of a storage closet. Her clothes and hair had caught fire, and though she'd managed to douse the flames, she'd already suffered serious burns.

If she was still breathing, Damon couldn't tell. He could only cradle her in his arms while he carried her to safety. Outside the burning lab, he collapsed and lay her on the floor. His damaged hands couldn't detect a pulse, but he put his lips against hers and breathed. "Come on, baby," he rasped. "Live, Miranda. Live."

The old images faded as Damon twisted in his sleep. But the nightmare wouldn't end. It merely transformed—into something hideous and ugly. Like him.

They were at the asylum now. Months later. Miranda's willowy figure was lost beneath the green hospital gown. And she was crying. At least, her shoulders moved with the sounds of sobbing. The tear ducts beneath the bandages that wrapped her face could no longer cry.

"Why won't you help me?" Her blue eyes pierced him straight to the core, adding to the weight of well-deserved guilt he carried. "How can you make yourself right and not help me?"

She should never have been a part of this. Miranda was an innocent pawn, caught and trampled by someone's jealous greed. If only he'd been an ordinary man. Less rich. Less powerful. Less of a visionary brainiac. None of this would have happened. His work wouldn't have been stolen. His lab wouldn't have been destroyed. She wouldn't have been hurt.

Damon Sinclair loved like an ordinary man, but he was cursed with being anything but.

"We nearly lost you in the E.R. when you reacted to the treatments. I won't risk that again until I run more experiments. For some reason the tissue regeneration formula doesn't work on you. I haven't figured out why. Yet. But I will. I promise." He joined her at the window. It was the last time he remembered feeling the heat of sunshine on his skin. "In the meantime, there's reconstructive surgery—"

"That takes too long. I'll never be the same."

He gently stroked her arm. "Money is no object. Whatever it takes. Whatever experts we need—"

"I thought you were the expert." She shrugged off his touch. "Your hands have healed. But my face…?"

Damon reached for her again, but she slid away, crossing to the far side of the small room whose posh amenities couldn't completely mask its clinical purpose. "Miranda, you are beautiful to me. Inside. Where it counts. I love you. I will always love you, no matter what."

"But I'm not beautiful outside anymore, am I?" She faced him then, the bandages masking everything but the accusation in her eyes. "You can't look at me and say I'm beautiful on the outside, can you?"

His medical breakthroughs weren't infallible. "I

can't fix my eye, either, and the nerve repair is still incom—"

"But you fixed the skin on your hands. What about the skin on my face? It's not vanity. It's humanity. I have no face left. No lips, no nose. Just…scars."

She hated him. So much. Where once he'd seen love, he saw nothing but blame and contempt. Hell, he hated himself. He'd worked miracles for so many patients. "Miranda—"

"Fix me, Damon. Fix me!"

"I don't know how." The admission twisted cruelly through a brain that had always had the answers. Always. Until now. "I don't know how."

"I don't know how," he muttered, finding no peace in slumber. "I don't know how!"

Damon lashed out at himself in his nightmare and awoke to the crash of glass.

He blinked his good eye into the glaring brightness of lights reflecting off stainless steel. Even as he pushed himself away from the lab table where he'd fallen asleep, the frustration and guilt that haunted his nightmares were still with him. He had a shattered petrie dish and contaminated solution on the floor by his feet, to boot. "Damn."

Another experiment gone to waste. Not that he'd expected this one to work better than any of the others he'd run in the last month. He didn't know if his equations were off, or if the sample had been tainted. But as he rolled the kinks from his neck and adjusted the black strap that crossed his forehead and held the patch over the empty socket where his left eye had been, he knew the answers would continue to elude him tonight.

A glance out the window of his twenty-eighth-floor lab told him it was well past midnight, even before he noted the time on the clock above the door. Time would forever be his enemy. No formula or device his clever mind could conjure would ever grant him the time he needed. The time he'd lost with Miranda.

Their marriage hadn't been perfect. He'd worked too much in the lab; she had loved to travel. But she'd given him a beautiful home life and a trusted voice in the Sinclair Pharmaceuticals office; he'd given her everything she'd asked for.

Except her humanity.

He hadn't found the answer to heal her in time. He hadn't made her feel whole again. He couldn't save her from her injuries—or the resulting depression. His skills weren't enough. His money wasn't enough.

His love wasn't enough.

Wide awake, as he searched for a broom and dustpan, he saw the vision—as clearly as he'd seen it that morning at the asylum.

Miranda. Dead.

An empty bottle of pills beside her on the bed.

No stomach pump, no science, no miracle could bring his wife back to him.

The note she'd left him had been brief.

D—
I can't do this anymore.
M.

Some lousy chromosome in her genetic makeup kept the miracle drugs that had earned his company millions from working. He'd even tested the tissue-regeneration formula on himself. The prototypes might be scarred and ugly, but he'd regained the use of his hands. The fingerprints hadn't all come back, but he had sensation in almost every nerve, and most of his dexterity had returned. He could do his work. He could type his notes and mix his chemicals and write his equations. He could feel heat and cold and pain.

God, yes. He was a pro at that now. Through and through. Some days, pain was all he could feel.

Damon paused in the center of his new lab. He pulled back the front of his white coat, propped his hands at his hips, tipped his head back and roared at the soundproof ceiling.

It wasn't fair that he should be alive while Miranda was dead. It wasn't fair that he should have more money than some small countries and not know happiness anymore. It wasn't fair that he couldn't find the solution to Miranda's Formula— the tissue-regenerating miracle intended to save patients who shared the same genetic predisposition she'd had.

He couldn't even honor her memory with that.

"So what are you going to do about it, Doc?" he asked aloud, breathing deeply and talking to himself in a way that had always cleared his thoughts and enabled him to concentrate. "For starters, I'm going to see if that persistent bastard has made any progress breaking into SinPharm's restricted files."

With something new to engage his brain, Damon was a happier man. He rolled a stool over to his computer and logged in to his company's database. In just a few keystrokes, he located the illegal activity and grinned. The nosy SOB was back. "Welcome, Mr. Black Hole of the Universe." Catchy online name. Appropriate since the hacker had tried a dozen different ways to download his research codes. In the middle of the night, when SinPharm's corporate offices were closed and the satellite labs and production facilities had been secured, someone was trying to hack into Damon's private files.

It had been another restless night a couple weeks back when he'd first detected the unknown computer geek trying to access his research through online channels. The hacker had broken in three different times to download codes that were misdirecting fakes to begin with. Once the false codes were applied to the data that had been stolen from his lab eighteen months ago, the thieves would realize that they'd been duped. Again. They'd wind up with cotton candy or a laxative—not any of his patented medicines or experimental drugs.

Though he'd had no luck tracing either the location or the identity of Black Hole yet, Damon had led the intruder on a merry chase. He sat and watched the screen as his opponent peeled away layer after layer of security protocols, getting closer to the translation codes that could turn Damon's equations from gibberish into millions of dollars.

And just when the perp was about to reach the innermost level, Damon pushed a button and scrambled the codes all over again.

His laughter was rare, a rusty sound that stretched the scarred muscles of his throat. SinPharm's security firm had their way of preventing industrial espionage, and Damon had his.

"That should keep you busy for a few more days." Hell, if the enemy wanted to reproduce his formulas and market competitive medical treatments without doing their own research, then they were damn well gonna have to get past him.

Unless he tracked them down first and introduced them to the FDA, the FCC and any other government organization whose laws they'd violated.

And if Damon discovered the hacker was in any way responsible for the theft and fire that led to Miranda's suicide, then he would personally put him out of business.

Permanently.

While he relished the image of the unknown spy throwing up his hands and cursing at the computer screen, Damon knew he had problems closer to home he needed to deal with. He glanced at the broken glass and dissipating chemical on the floor. "Like you."

Damon rolled his stool over to another desk, where two rows of monitors helped him keep an eye on the Sinclair Tower through adjustable interior and exterior security cameras. He typed in a command and brought up a view of the main rooms in the penthouse upstairs. Good. All was quiet. His housekeeper's seemingly intuitive ability to know when he'd screwed up and needed a little extra help hadn't awakened her from her sleep.

But by morning, if he didn't clean it up tonight, then she'd somehow know. She'd be down here at first light, cleaning and tutting herself into a worried state until she verified for herself that he hadn't been cut or injured in any way.

Corporate spies he could handle. But it was funny how such a tiny little woman, who'd once changed his diapers and sent him to his room, could transform six feet, three inches of brains and testosterone into a guilty little boy, as eager to please as he was to cover his tracks and stay out of trouble with her.

But the bonded cleaning crew he hired to sterilize the lab once a week brought their own supplies, and if there was a broom to be had, he wasn't finding it.

Mental note: buy cleaning supplies for the lab.

In the meantime, he could raid his housekeeper's private stash. Damon draped his lab coat over a hook beside the rear exit, swiped his key card through the lock and hurried up the back stairs to the penthouse where they lived on the top two floors.

His plan was simple: sneak into her unguarded kitchen to borrow a broom and dustpan, then dispose of the evidence and hide the fact that he'd spent yet another sleep-deprived night working in his lab.

Yet as he tiptoed past the darkened hallway that led to her quarters, something made Damon stop. Everything was as neat and tidy as it had appeared on the monitor downstairs. But something was off. Perhaps it was the absence of any familiar sound that pricked his senses and put him on alert.

There was no humidifier running, no television chattering on after his housekeeper had fallen asleep. He heard no soft, denasal snore. Damon leaned the broom and dustpan against the wall, turned the corner and gently knocked on her door.

There was no answer. The woman had raised him after his mother's death, had stayed on after his marriage. She'd been there through his father's passing. Had remained with him past her own retirement, the accident and Miranda's suicide. They were as close to being a family as two people who shared no bloodline could be. Squashing a flare of panic beneath cold, rational purpose, Damon opened the bedroom door to check on her.

"Helen?"

"Miss Snow?" A nurse joined Kit at the ICU window, looking through the criss-crossed steel filaments inside the glass to the fragile, wan woman in the hospital bed on the other side.

"There's no change, is there." Kit had stayed as close as the hospital staff would allow while surgical and neurological teams stitched up the elderly woman's head wound, monitored cranial pressure and vital signs, and tucked her into the sterile room for observation. Until she regained consciousness, there was no way for the doctors to completely assess how much damage the three attackers had done. No way for the police to get any more information on the mugging beyond Kit's concise—but all too incomplete—statement.

"We're doing everything we can." The plump nurse shrugged. "The rest is up to her."

The mysterious Helen didn't look strong enough to fight off a pesky fly, much less fight for her life. *We're all dead?*

Where was the hope in that? Was that going to be Helen's last, despairing thought? Kit splayed her fingers at the edge of the cool glass, wishing she could hold Helen's thin, bony hand again, and share whatever warmth and encouragement the woman needed to survive. Truman Medical Center was already a dim, ominously quiet tomb at three in the morning. Walking away and leaving the elderly woman in the care of staff who knew even less about her than Kit did felt like abandonment.

Kit's parents had been found holding hands when their bodies were discovered after the fire, with debris from the explosion blocking their escape. According to the arson team who'd combed through the diner afterward, Matthew and Phyllis Snow had most likely succumbed to the toxic smoke long before they'd been burned or crushed by the collapsing ceiling. But they'd had each other—they'd known love and a hopeful connection to something outside themselves—right until the end of their lives.

Kit curled her fingers into a fist. Someone

should be in there, holding Helen's hand, giving her hope. "She shouldn't be alone."

But the nurse hadn't come to give a medical report, and she had no clue about Kit's frustrated sense of justice for all. "It's long past visiting hours. And since you're not family, well…I'm sorry." Her apologetic frown didn't ease the sting of dismissal. "Our Jane Doe needs her rest."

"She's not a Jane Doe," Kit insisted, fighting for her neighbor the only way she could. "Her name's Helen. She lives in the Sinclair Building. You put *Helen* on her charts, didn't you? I can't imagine how disoriented she'd feel if she woke up and you started calling her by someone else's name."

"Yes. We have her listed as Helen Doe. Sorry to alarm you. We passed along all the information you gave us to the police. I'm sure they're checking their missing persons files right now." The nurse's rueful sigh recaptured Kit's attention. "Go home. It's late. You've already done more for her than most Good Samaritans would."

"Someone had to be here to answer questions." That was the practical excuse she'd given for climbing into the ambulance while the paramedics worked on Helen.

"I heard you chased away her attackers. It's all over the hospital. She might be dead if it wasn't for you."

"That's not why I'm here." Kit had left Germane back at the diner to wait until Matt showed up. She intended to call him before she left, to see if her brother had gotten home safely. In the meantime, Helen's needs had been more pressing. Kit had held the older woman's chilly hand until the staff chased her away. Now all she could do was keep her distance and watch and wait. "People shouldn't be alone. Especially when they're hurting or afraid. Someone needs to be here for her."

Her brother might not appreciate her vigilance. The neighborhood might think her more busy-body than philanthropist. But the unconscious Helen couldn't stop her from caring.

The nurse nudged her toward the lobby. "One of the staff will check her regularly throughout the night. But until we get word from her family, or visiting hours resume at 9:00 a.m. tomorrow, I'm afraid you'll have to wait someplace else."

Kit exhaled a deep breath and finally acknowledged the aches and fatigue of her own banged-up body. "I should have lied and said I was her granddaughter, shouldn't I?"

The nurse offered a sympathetic smile. "Come back in the morning. You need your rest as much as she does."

Without further argument, Kit nodded and dragged her feet toward the deserted lobby. Since she hadn't paused to grab her purse before climbing into the ambulance, Kit's cell phone was still back at the diner. Posted signs warned her she wasn't allowed to use her cell on the ICU floor, anyway, but out here she could access a bank of landline telephones to call Germane and Matt.

Maybe she should phone for a cab instead, and head on home as the nurse had suggested. After a few hours' sleep, she could search out which apartments above her were occupied, and start knocking on doors. Other than the model apartments, the rooms above the fifth floor weren't finished. But someone had to know Helen. Maybe one of the construction workers had met her and could provide some information. Kit would ask them when they came in for lunch the next day.

But the cops were probably already going through the building tonight. Hopefully, they'd have better luck getting hold of her landlord at Sinclair Pharmaceuticals than she'd ever had, as well. Though she'd never had any contact with the man beyond letters and leases and rent checks, Easting Davitz, Esq., had her entire financial history on file. Chances were he'd have files on the other tenants, as well.

And, if the cops and Mr. Davitz couldn't find out anything more about Helen, Kit would still have plenty of time to come back to the hospital to visit in the morning. She could spend a couple of hours holding the woman's hand—maybe read a book or just talk—before she had to get the ovens fired up and the diner opened for lunch at eleven.

With that much of a plan giving her legs a reason to move, Kit picked up the receiver on the first wall phone and deposited fifty cents. When Germane's cell number kicked her over to his voice mail, she hung up and called Matt directly. When his voice mail answered, Kit spoke the familiar words. "Matt? It's way past curfew. If you're there, pick up. I just need to know you're okay. I'll see you at work tomorrow. Right?" If she was lucky. "I just need you to answer me and let me know you're safe."

Of course no one answered. Matt didn't seem to answer to anyone these days. When the recorder beeped, Kit hung up.

Maybe Matt had gotten home and Germane was hanging out with him at the apartment until she returned. Maybe he hadn't shown up at all and Germane had gone out to look for him. Matt was *her* brother. *She* should be the one out searching—not her sixty-year-old Dutch uncle with arthritic knees.

Buzzing her lips to dispel a gathering tension, Kit dipped into her jeans pockets to find more change. She pulled out several folded dollar bills from the tips she'd jammed inside. But change for a single phone call? She found one quarter.

"Come on." Fatigue made her easily frustrated. All she wanted was to ensure Matt was okay and that Germane wasn't doing anything foolish. Kit set the coin on the counter and dug for more. A measly dime. A movie ticket stub that had gone through the laundry. A penny. "I thought you were supposed to be lucky."

Kit swallowed hard, squelching the sarcastic thought. The Snows made their own luck. They took care of what needed to be taken care of without some random flip of a coin to make their lives easier or not. But she was getting a little tired of being stuck in the "or not" category. She glanced toward the nurses' station, wondering if they could make some change for her. But the desk had been deserted by the skeleton staff out making their rounds.

With her pockets practically empty and her patience wearing thin, Kit decided she was just going to have to hike downstairs to the main lobby. If she couldn't make a call there, then she'd hail a cab. Of course, the pitiful sum lying on the counter beneath the phone wouldn't get her two city blocks, much less back to the heart of downtown. And without the coat she'd left back at the diner, it would be a mighty cold walk home. Maybe Tariq would do her a favor and let her ride for free. But she couldn't even make that call without another quarter for the phone.

Her shoulders stiffened with an unconscious bracing that was almost as second nature as breathing. This wouldn't be the first time she'd had to find her way home at night. Alone. On foot. She'd spent too many nights out looking for a brother who just couldn't seem to forgive the world and grow up. "Be there, Matty," she prayed, scraping the cash back into her pocket and pulling the receiver from her ear. "Please be there."

"Operator. May I help you?"

"What?" Hallelujah! Kit quickly drew the friendly voice back to her ear. "Yes. I have an emergency. Of sorts. I'm at Truman Medical Center, and I need to call home to make sure everyone's all right. At the very least, I need to call for a ride, but I don't have the right change. I know it's late…"

The operator didn't need to hear any more excuses. "In the event of an emergency, you can reach the phone company by dialing zero. No charge for a limited call. What number are you trying to reach?"

Kit recited the number for her apartment, thanked the operator and tapped an anxious foot in time with the ringing of the phone. It was hard to block the unsettling images that were half memory, half imagination. Her waiting at the police station to post bail. Matt turning his back on her and walking away when she wanted to hug him in her arms and keep him close. The three muggers returning to the scene of the crime and breaking into the diner. Meeting Matt on the street. Forcing him to join their little crime spree. Or worse—making him their next victim.

Kit shifted on her feet, hating how easy it had become to imagine the worst. "C'mon, guys. Pick up."

Her home number rang three times. Four.

A crackle of static buzzed in her ear, and the line went dead.

"Limited call, my ass." Kit jiggled the disconnect button, trying to get a dial tone again. "Operator? Op—?"

Every light on the floor went out, plunging her into darkness. Kit grabbed the edge of the counter, anchoring herself in the sudden, disorienting abyss. "What the heck?"

Almost instantly, a hum of disembodied voices and quick movement rolled down the hallways from the patients' rooms. But they sounded far away from the bubble of black silence that engulfed her in the lobby.

An uneasy fear quickly replaced her frustration. "Hello?"

She'd welcome any answer from the phone or the nurses' station. But, blinded by the instant night, Kit didn't know where to turn. Which distant voice to call to.

"Where's that backup?"

"Ten-second delay."

"Check every patient."

"Why does this always happen at night?"

"Critical systems are still online."

Kit curled her toes into her boots, staying put out of the staff's way. She clutched the dead receiver to her chest and held on, counting off an eternity until those ten seconds passed and the backup generators kicked on.

...two one-thousand, three one-thousand...

A breeze swept across the back of her neck, raising goose bumps beneath her ponytail. Someone was right here.

Before she could turn around, a gloved hand clamped over her mouth. In the same instant a strong arm looped around her waist and dragged her back against an unyielding chest. Kit screamed behind the muzzle and twisted in her assailant's grasp.

"Shh. Be still," a deep voice grated against her ear.

Still? Like hell.

Kit threw down the phone and clawed at the glove. The leather was soft, supple, warm. But the hand inside wouldn't budge. Protests rang inside her ears but found no outlet. Had the mugger in the Chiefs parka followed her to the hospital? Was this surprise attack his way of keeping her from saying anything to the police?

Man, had he picked the wrong cookie to mess with.

She kicked at an instep, braced her foot against the wall and tried to shove him off balance. His arm slipped, then grabbed again, hooking beneath the swell of her breasts. When he fought to regain his hold on her, he palmed one feminine mound and squeezed. Even through layers of a sweater and glove, Kit lurched at the contact, alarmed as heat bloomed beneath his way too personal grasp. The man cursed and jerked his hand away. A surer grip tightened around her jaw, stifling any cry for help. Then, just as she thought she might wiggle her way free, the vise of hard arm and harder body lifted her clear off the floor. He carried her forward a step, pinning her between the counter and the wall of his chest.

"I said be still." The lips that brushed the warning against her neck startled her into silence as much as the man's alarming strength did. His hips cupped her bottom, his thighs pressed into hers. His moist breath burned a path behind the shell of her ear. Kit held her breath. *Oh, God. What did he want from her? What did he—* "I won't hurt you," the gravelly voice promised. "I just need you to listen."

Understanding the unspoken bargain that co-operation was her best deterrent against more unwanted gropes and her only chance at freedom, Kit nodded.

Suspended in the darkness, deprived of sight, Kit could do little but absorb the impressions of heat and masculinity that bombarded her senses. He wasn't the same man who'd attacked Helen. There was no trace of an accent in his unusual voice. He wore a tailored leather coat, not a parka. He was too tall to be the mugger's sidekick. And while he could have been the third man who'd thrown her up against the wall, she was beginning to think this guy had a different purpose beyond intimidation. The men in the alley had been more than willing to hurt her. And though there was something disturbingly intimate about being pressed shoulder-to-thigh against a stranger in the darkness, this man made no effort to take advantage of her vulnerable position.

That wasn't the only detail she noticed.

With every deepening breath, Kit inhaled medicinal soap and leather, along with the odd scent of roses. Though shadowy in form, there was no mistaking the reality and substance of this man. He was lanky. Long-limbed. Solid. The crisp chill of winter clung to his coat, but his mouth radiated a heat against her skin that was dangerously enticing. The beeps of distant monitors chirped in the distance, but it was the gravelly husk of his low-pitched whisper that commanded her attention.

"Thank you for taking care of Helen."

Helen? He knew Helen? Kit mumbled the question against his hand.

"I will repay my debt to you."

Her toes touched the floor as he released his grip on her. Kit sucked in a deep breath and worked the stiffness from her jaw. "What debt? Who—"

"No. Don't turn around." A large palm at the center of her back seared her to the bone. The heat of that firm, commanding touch was enough to hold her in place. "Don't."

Kit pressed her lips together and peered straight ahead into the darkness. A chill swept in and raised goose bumps beneath her sweater as his hand left her. Hadn't ten seconds passed yet? Or had she lost all track of time the instant her vision had failed her?

"I don't want your money. Who are you?" The heat was gone. *He* was gone. "Wait." Ignoring his order, Kit whirled around.

Ten.

Emergency lights flickered on, bathing the lobby and hallways with a greenish glow. Kit blinked until her eyes adjusted to the eerie twilight. "Hey." What happened to Tall, Dark and Creepy? "Mister?"

She thought she caught a glimpse of black stealing around the corner. The sweep of movement was longer and more flowing than the white coats and colorful uniforms of the nurses and staff. Kit hurried after it. "Wait. Tell me about Helen. The hospital needs to know her last name and address."

By the time she skirted the corner, the shadowy figure had vanished. "No way."

The dead-end hallway was empty. The door to a utility closet stood ajar and Kit peeked inside. Nothing.

Almost nothing.

She squinted as a small box on the closet's back wall caught her eye. Kit touched it with her fingertips, then flinched from its ticking pulse. It was some sort of timer linked to an electrical conduit. Was it just an unlikely coincidence that this door stood open? Was that box part of the backup generator system? Or had the man with the ruined voice done something to the power grid? Why? Surely not just to cop a free feel and thank her for being a good neighbor to Helen.

Helen.

With suspicion thumping her heart against her chest, Kit ran back the opposite direction, past the warning call of the attending nurse, back to the ICU rooms. "Helen?"

The white-haired woman still lay in her bed,

unmoved, unconscious. But there was something different, something out of place. Kit zeroed in on the unexpected spot of color on the white blanket.

"What is going on?" Kit's whisper fogged the viewing window.

Instead of wiping it clear, she pushed open the door and went inside the chilled room for a closer look. A single pink long-stemmed rose lay next to Helen's hand. The familiar scent and suspicious timing told Kit that *he* had brought the flower, and that the dark, powerful scrawl on the card tied to the rose was *his*.

Kit leaned in closer to decipher the handwriting in the dim light. "Helen Hodges. Age: 72. Allergies: Penicillin." The back side of the card listed medications for asthma and arthritis, as well as an insurance number.

"Not much of a romantic, is he." But definitely someone who cared enough to ensure that Helen Hodges received the proper treatment. Someone who cared, period. Kit wrapped her fingers around the woman's fragile hand. "Who was he, Helen?"

Who was the secretive man with the warm lips and ruined voice?

A son who had an aversion to hospitals, perhaps? A grandson who preferred the darkness? A lawyer or accountant who was afraid he'd get stuck with the hospital bill if he was seen?

"Is he a criminal? Ex-husband?" No. His body

had been too young and strong to be a contemporary of Helen's. "Is he part owl or bat?"

But Kit's tired attempt at humor couldn't even elicit her own smile. "Do you even know he was here?"

The pale, expressionless face gave no answer.

A sweep of warmer air told Kit the door had opened behind her. She stiffened for a moment, then relaxed, quickly ascertaining that *he* hadn't returned.

"You need to leave, Miss Snow." Judging by the sharp tone, any sympathy the nurse had felt for Kit's persistent vigil had worn off. "We can't have anyone extra in the way when the main power's off-line like this."

"The monitors never stopped working, did they?" Kit was thinking out loud as much as asking a question. "He didn't jeopardize the patients. He just wanted to remain anonymous."

But why?

Why?

"He?" the nurse asked.

"You didn't see anyone besides me come into this room, did you?" But Kit already knew the answer was no.

"Good night, Miss Snow."

Kit acknowledged the dismissal with a nod. "Her name is Helen Hodges. There's health information on the card here. I'd double check everything, of course, but I have a feeling it's accurate."

"Now."

Pulling the rose's soft bud into Helen's palm, Kit closed her slender fingers around it. "He must care about you an awful lot to go to all this trouble." The nurse cleared her throat and Kit raised her hands in surrender. "I'm going. I'm going."

As soon as Kit stepped outside the door, every light on the floor flashed back on. She reached for a wall and braced herself while her eyes read-justed to the harsh intrusion of brightness. First the darkness had blinded her, and now the sudden glare rendered her just as helpless.

A perfect diversion.

"Damn."

Curious to know more about the man who'd grabbed her like an attacker while insisting he meant her no harm, Kit hurried to the lobby. Empty. No one but uniformed staff prowled the hallways. She went back to the utility closet to inspect her only clue to the man's appearance and mysterious vanishing act.

But the timing device had disappeared now, as well.

She could almost chalk up the entire incident as a fantasy of her weary imagination. The blackout had lasted a matter of seconds. The backup lights had run just a minute or two longer. Everything was back to normal. Back to quiet. Back to her being alone in the middle of the night without the change to call home.

Then she detected it. The lingering scents of leather and soap stirred her pulse. That man—Helen's unseen friend—had been in here. He had caused that precise, patient-friendly power outage.

Kit strolled back to the phones, trying to organize her observations into a pattern that made sense. The man in the leather coat and gloves had sought her out in the darkness for a reason. He'd come to see Helen. But he'd come for Kit, too.

She caught her breath and froze, knowing for certain that their meeting hadn't been accidental.

I will repay my debt.

And Kit had a funny feeling he wasn't talking about the stack of quarters scattered across the telephone counter in the lobby.

Chapter Three

"Where were you last night?" Kit looked up from her bowl of soggy cereal and glared at the eighteen-year-old with the spiked golden-brown hair and the annoyingly alert blue gaze, so unlike her own sleep-deprived eyes. Man, the kid had gall.

As relieved as she'd been to find Matt asleep in his bed when Tariq had finally dropped her off at four this morning, Kit suspected her brother's loud snore had been a ruse to keep her from asking any questions. Granting them both a couple hours of peace, she'd turned off the bedside lamp, planted a kiss on his cheek and silently promised that once she got a little rest and felt slightly more human, a conversation was going to happen.

Welcome to slightly more human.

"I was at the hospital." Needing something with a little more crunch to sustain her, Kit carried her bowl to the sink and reached for an apple from the basket of fruit on the counter. Kit hissed at the pain that stabbed through her shoulder, and quickly pulled her arm back to her side. "Wow."

"Kit? You okay?" Was that concern she heard in Matt's voice? When she turned around, she caught a glimpse of the sweet baby brother she'd once been so close to. But his I-don't-give-a-damn mask slipped back into place before she could relish the connection. He stuffed a spoonful of cereal into his mouth and chewed around the matter-of-fact question. "Did you get hurt?"

The fist-size bruise that had turned her right collar bone and shoulder joint an ugly shade of purple was apparently going to limit her flexibility for the next few days. But, like the other bumps and aches on her body, it wasn't going to stop her from looking out for her brother and taking care of the business that needed to be handled today.

"I wasn't the patient." She purposefully gritted her teeth and picked up an apple before pulling out a paring knife and returning to the table. She offered Matt the first wedge of fruit. "Want some?"

"I'm good."

Fine. Don't even let me feed you. Kit popped the apple slice into her mouth and continued carving. "Actually, I was there for a neighbor of ours. Helen Hodges?"

Matt downed the last of his milk. "The old lady who lives upstairs?"

Surprise, surprise. "You know her?"

"Not really." When he started to leave the kitchen, Kit reminded him to rinse his dishes and put them in the dishwasher. With a grunt of acquiescence he went to the sink and did as she asked. "I bussed her table a couple of times when she was in the diner. She slipped me a tip because she said the waitresses don't always share with the guys who clear the tables."

"She gave you money?"

"Yeah. Twenty bucks one time. I guess she had it to spare. She said to use it for school or to put gas in my car." Matt turned and rolled his eyes, reminding Kit what a touchy subject that was. "If I had one."

"I'm sorry that putting off buying a car is a sacrifice we had to make. I figured it was more important to keep a roof over your head. You know you can borrow mine if something important comes up. In the meantime, I'm saving, you're saving—"

"When, Kit?"

"It's not that big a hardship to be without a car right now. You work right here, you take the bus to school—"

"What about when I go to college? I'm not taking the bus to California."

Kit counted off a couple of beats so she wouldn't jump at the topic. "Are you still planning to go?"

She counted off two more before pointing out, "If you don't get your grades back up this semester, you'll probably lose your scholarship. And you can't raise those grades if you're out all hours of the night and missing classes and not getting your work done. You've got a real gift, Matt, as smart as you are. I hate to see you throwing it all away."

No comment.

She stuck the knife into the core of the apple to keep it safely away from her tense fingers. She had to ask. "Where were *you* last night? Say, after midnight? Two hours past when I asked you to be home?"

Matt's to-hell-with-it grin warned her she wasn't going to get any useful answers. "With friends."

"What friends?"

"You wouldn't know them."

"I should. Invite them over sometime."

"To do what? Wash dishes?"

"They could eat. I'd be happy to feed them." Kit rose and joined him at the sink. "I thought you liked doing those fix-it projects around the apartment and diner. Do any of your friends enjoy tearing things apart and rebuilding them the way you do?"

He rolled his eyes. "Right. I'm gonna invite someone over to fix the toaster."

She had to give him that one. "Okay, so that

wouldn't be my first choice for a fun night out, either. What sorts of things do you do with these friends I don't know?"

"Play games, mostly."

"Where?"

He slammed the door of the dishwasher shut. "Dammit, Kit, Mom and Dad never grilled me like this!"

She flinched at his burst of temper, but swallowed hard to keep her cool. That was pain she saw in the tight press of his mouth. The angry glare in his eyes was just the mask that couldn't quite hide the truth. She wanted to reach up and touch his scruffy cheek. But somehow she had become the enemy and she wasn't sure her comfort would be welcomed, so she stuck her fists down into the pockets of her robe instead. "They had seventeen years' experience taking care of you—I'm new at this. I'm doing my best. I wish you'd help me, not work against me. You never acted like this when Mom and Dad were around."

"Yeah, well, they're not here, are they?" He scowled down at her.

"The diner is our home—"

"This place killed them!" He raked his fingers through his permanently unruly hair and stalked across the room. "You don't know what it was like. You weren't here to see them…like that.

They were trapped. All the exits were blocked. There was nothing they could do *but* die."

"Matt." Enemy or not, Kit hurried across the room and wrapped her arms around his waist. He stiffly refused to respond, but when he didn't pull away, Kit held on. "It was a terrible loss, a tragic accident. But it wasn't anybody's fault. I promise you, those smoke alarms and CO_2 detectors you installed will give us all the warning we need. And Mr. Kronemeyer's crew is putting sprinkler systems throughout the building. We'll be perfectly safe."

With a scoffing laugh, he pulled away. "A few gadgets won't make things right. Haven't you noticed things have changed since we were kids? You were gone for six years, sis. This isn't the same place you left behind."

"I know the neighborhood has gone downhill. But there are still good people here. You have to believe in that." She wanted him to believe in her, in them. "It will never be the same without Mom and Dad. But you and I are still a family. We have to talk to each other. We need to be able to trust each other."

"I need to get to school."

Cinching the pink chenille tie tighter around her waist, Kit followed him to the back door where he shrugged into a sheepskin coat with frayed sleeves that were too short for his arms. "Where's your new coat? The Chiefs jacket I gave you for Christmas?"

"Don't know."

"You don't know? I spent a small fortune on that thing. It was what you wanted." *I know, I know.* "Besides a car. So what happened to it?"

He hauled his book bag up onto his shoulder. "I'll get it back."

"That's not what I asked." She pulled the knit scarf he'd left behind off its hook and looped it around his neck. "Matt, last night Helen Hodges was attacked in the alley. The man who hurt her was wearing a red-and-gold Chiefs parka."

He shooed her hands away. "So now you think I'm beating up old ladies in the alley?"

She hated to admit that, for a split second, the possibility had crossed her mind last night. She prayed she knew her brother better than that. "Of course it wasn't you. But if she was handing out large chunks of cash, you might have told someone. Maybe the same someone you loaned your coat to?"

"No, he wouldn't do that."

"Who, Matt?" She retreated from the blast of cold air that hit her when he opened the back door. "I'm not accusing you of anything. I'm trying to understand why someone would hurt that woman. And why no one but…" She shook her head to dispel the vivid tactile memories that flooded her body with heat. *I will repay my debt to you.* She wasn't ready to mention the tall, gruff-voiced mystery man at the hospital, or else *she'd* sound like the crazy, irresponsible sibling. "I'm trying to understand why no one seems to know her or where she lives. Why your coat may have been worn by one of the men who attacked her. Who attacked *me!* If you have answers, I want to hear them."

"So you can report me to the police? I didn't do anything wrong last night."

"But you won't say what you *were* doing. Or who you were doing it with." Kit grabbed on to the door and asked again. "What happened to your coat?"

"I have to get to school. Before you jump my case about that, too."

"Matt." He was out the door. Kit stepped out onto the concrete stoop to keep his long, lazy stride in sight. "I need you at work at four-thirty. And tomorrow morning you meet with your counselor. I expect you to keep the appointment this week."

"Yeah, yeah," he muttered, ducking beneath the steel scaffolding and heading toward the street.

"And pull up your pants. There's a dress code at school, remember? You've got a cute butt— you should show it off." Even that teasing truth failed to get any more talk out of him. He was leaving without a backward glance. Flannel pajamas couldn't keep the wintry breeze from blowing against her skin and raising goose bumps. "I love you."

But he was gone. Kit hugged her arms around her middle and shivered. Cold as she was, alone as she felt, there was an odd heat centered between her shoulder blades that caused her to turn around and peer into the empty expanse of the alley behind her.

Maybe not so alone.

Was someone watching her? Had one of the workmen come early? Right. Like flannel pj's and fuzzy slippers would merit a whistle or two.

She lifted her gaze to the parking garage on the opposite side. There weren't even any cars moving there yet. There was no one else here. She was safe.

Getting grabbed from behind twice in the same morning made her paranoid, that was all.

Still, Kit hurried inside, unable to shake the eerie feeling of being watched until she locked the door behind her. Releasing the breath she didn't know she'd been holding, she hustled her own butt to get showered and dressed and off to explore the building before visiting Helen.

Helen Hodges hadn't just formed out of the mist. There had to be a tangible clue somewhere in the Sinclair Tower that would let Kit know where the woman belonged. There had to be something to tell her more about the mystery man she seemed to belong to.

WHAT WAS THAT WOMAN up to?

Damon propped his feet on the desk and leaned back, sipping his coffee and watching his first-floor neighbor chatting up the construction crew on a row of monitors. She'd already walked the halls on three floors, peeked into unused offices and invited herself into one of the model apartments.

She was certainly a curious specimen. Thorough and methodical in a way that Damon could relate to—friendly and outgoing in a way he was not. But what was she looking for? Though he couldn't hear the words, he could read the nonverbal cues of posture and gestures, and tell she was asking questions.

About what? The building? The remodel? The attack? Helen? Him?

If he'd had half of this high-tech, personally enhanced security system installed throughout the building eighteen months ago, he'd have seen the enemy coming that night. He'd still have his original notes. He wouldn't have had to build a new lab or play games with that hacker. He'd have the full use of two good hands and both eyes.

His wife wouldn't be dead.

Damon inhaled deeply, carefully controlling his

emotional response to all he had lost. He no longer allowed his thoughts to be clouded by sentimental attachments. Beyond Helen, of course.

That was excuse enough to acquaint himself with his first-floor neighbor. Helen would want to thank her, want to do something kind and generous to repay her. But until his housekeeper regained consciousness, Damon would evaluate this would-be friend for her. Though his security cameras had caught the vicious, faceless attackers on tape, Damon had seen the danger too late. Caught up in the throes of his nightmares, he'd failed to protect Helen when she'd needed him most.

He wouldn't fail to protect her again.

If his first-floor neighbor proved to be as straightforward and caring as she appeared to be, then Damon would personally write a check for whatever thank-you gift Helen wished to bestow on her. But if she'd discovered Helen's connection to the wealthy SinPharm empire and intended to take advantage of her grateful nature, then he'd have his executive liaison, Easting Davitz, close the woman's restaurant and kick her out of the building.

But for now he was content to collect data and observe the subject in question. He'd organize the facts and determine his opinion of her later.

He already knew everything about Katherine Elizabeth Snow that a piece of paper could tell him. He set his coffee mug down on the stack of information his security team had pulled for him this morning. The printout said she was twenty-six, never married, had one brother in high school, and was a partner in a restaurant business she'd inherited from her late parents. She stood five-six, weighed a healthy 130 pounds, and was a practicum short of earning a Masters in criminal justice studies to go with her chemistry degree from Central Missouri State University.

As he watched her wave goodbye to the workers, he added a couple more facts to his list. Katherine Snow made people smile, and her worn blue jeans hugged a sweet, round bottom that was every bit as firm and sexy to look at as it had been to press against in the hospital lobby last night.

Damon jerked as if an unseen hand had slapped him in the face. Damn. Where had that thought come from?

"What are you thinking, Doc?" He warned himself away from the random memory that snuck in from his subconscious mind. Last night's tussle had been about communication and maintaining his anonymity—not whether or not a thirty-nine-year-old man could still get his rocks off with a woman after more than a year of mourning and celibacy.

But before Damon could get his focus back around the fact that he was spying on Katherine

Snow for Helen's sake, and not his own baser interests, she disappeared into the stairwell, capturing his curiosity in a different way. "Now what?" He drifted closer to the monitor. "Where are you going?"

Mental note: add security cameras to stairwell.

He didn't like being at a disadvantage, but instead of standing there like some adolescent fool, damning his left hand for having just enough functional nerve endings to remember what the swell of her breast had felt like in his unintended grasp, Damon turned his attention to a more familiar purpose. He crossed the lab and shut off the Bunsen burner beneath the variable ingredient of this morning's test formula. The liquid was hot enough to destabilize the molecules and recombine them with the regeneration mixture he'd already synthesized. When the new formula cooled, he'd add it to a petri dish along with a few skin cells from a volunteer subject who shared the same allergic predisposition Miranda had exhibited, and see if normal, viable tissue would grow.

This time Miranda's Formula would work.

"That's right, Doc. Jinx it." Inhaling deeply, Damon buried that twinge of emotion and turned his back on his work. He didn't believe much in the power of positive thinking anymore. He believed in cold, hard facts. Either the formula would work or it wouldn't. But he refused to hope.

Time to return to the security monitors and the less formal experiment at hand—his observational study of Katherine Snow. This time, he swore to remain purely objective.

But there was still no sign of her on any of the screens.

"Where are you?" An educated guess would indicate she'd continue her previous pattern and climb the stairs to the fifth floor. But unless she'd twisted an ankle, she should have shown up by now. "Unpredictable, hmm?"

Odd for a scientist. Maybe she was following some logical pattern of her own design. Unexpected. But far more engaging than waiting for a mixture to cool.

With a few quick keystrokes on the computer, he pulled up the cameras for the sixth and seventh floors. With no movement detected on either level, Damon switched to views of the lower floors. There was plenty of activity to observe in the lobby, where his current contractor, J. T. Kronemeyer, was arguing on the phone wedged between his shoulder and ear, and handing out assignments to his foremen.

But no Katherine Snow.

Damon typed in more commands. He accepted the challenge she unknowingly presented. "I'll find you."

Eighth floor, ninth floor. Where had she gone?

He absently massaged his brow bone, easing the phantom eye strain that settled behind the patch masking the left side of his face. "Come out, come out, wherever you…" Damon smiled and blew up the image on screen three. "Gotcha."

Breathing deeply after what must have been a quick, steady climb, his subject stepped out into the hallway on the thirteenth floor.

Feeling something akin to victory coursing through his veins, Damon raised his mug to his unwitting opponent and drained the last of his coffee. As he watched Katherine Snow squat down to study something on the tile floor, her quizzical expression piqued his own curiosity.

What was she doing on a cordoned-off floor, anyway? One that Kronemeyer's renovation crews hadn't even gotten to yet? The previous company Easting had hired, and subsequently fired for too many delays and "misplaced" supplies, had replaced the exterior windows, stripped the doors and added structural reinforcements to bring the settling walls up to code. But the thirteenth floor belonged to a different phase of the remodeling project. It wouldn't see any finishing work for several months. Miss Snow had no business being there.

Yet there was something beyond his camera angle that caught her eye. She stood and made the odd choice to walk along the edge of the tiled hallway. Why not take the middle path others had used?

Others?

"Curious." Damon typed as he sank onto the stool in front of the monitors. Was that…? He squinted his good eye and blew up the image on the screen. Footprints. In the thick layer of plaster dust that coated the floor. Fresh prints. Recent.

And Katherine Snow was following them.

"No, no," he admonished the monitor, wishing he could transmit some sort of telepathic warning to her. "You don't belong there."

Neither did the footprints.

"Be smart. Go back." Damon was already shrugging out of his lab coat. Had she heard a sound earlier? Was she following someone? Before any definitive answers could form, she turned a corner and disappeared from sight. "Damn." He tossed the coat and pulled up the next camera to find a shot of her. "Come back to me." He was searching. Searching. "C'mon."

Was that a door? Two? Three, hanging back in place? As Damon panned down the hallway, he discovered that some unsanctioned work had taken place. Floors thirteen through twenty-five should have been stripped down to bare bones. No way had Kronemeyer's crew gotten ahead of schedule. Since that electrician's unfortunate death, the missing crew member and the superstitious rumblings about the curse of landing a job at the Sinclair Tower, Kronemeyer's men couldn't even catch up. So who'd authorized replacing the doors?

"Where are you? Yes!" Damon shook a triumphant fist when her fresh-scrubbed face reappeared.

She was trailing her fingers along the wall, slowing her step as she reached the second door. Damon's pulse quickened to a bolder beat, feeling the same edgy anticipation reflected on her face.

"Don't do it." But his fingers were turning in the air, right along with hers, as she reached for the doorknob. He was just as curious as she to know what lay on the other side.

The instant the door swung open, two arms snaked out and latched on to her wrist.

Damon jumped. "What the hell?"

Man's hands. Suit-coat sleeves. Dragging her into the room out of the camera shot.

Damon cursed and ran from the lab. He swiped his key card through the security lock that accessed his private elevator and typed in the activation code. Once in, he pressed thirteen over and over until the doors slid shut.

Objectivity be damned. Katherine Snow was in trouble.

And he owed it to Helen to keep her safe.

Chapter Four

Grubby hands closed over her wrist and Kit screamed.

"Shh! Get in here," a strident voice whispered.

"Let go of me!" The door slammed. The hands dragged Kit to the center of the room. She stumbled over a bunched-up rug. The foul odor of sweat and booze stung her nose, granting her recognition an instant before her assailant released the hard pinch on her bones. "Henry!"

"Shh." The old man with the grizzled face and bulbous nose urged her aside with a placating hand. He blinked his watery eyes, trying to decide which one to spy through the peephole with. "I'm planning a surprise."

She'd certainly gotten one.

Relief surged through Kit, replacing panic with confusion and concern. This was definitely not what she'd expected to find in her search for Helen Hodges's apartment. Rubbing the chafe marks on her wrist, she assessed Henry Phipps's frayed, wrinkled suit and distant expression, and wondered how an addled old man could have such a painful grip. "You can't just grab someone like that. I thought I was being abducted."

Now that she knew she was in no real danger, Kit took a closer look at her surroundings. The apartment walls had been stripped down to its two-by-fours, revealing hanging wires and rusted switch boxes that looked as though they hadn't been functional for years. And though the window overlooking the parking garage still bore its factory sticker, there was nothing else new or clean about the rooms. A trio of well-worn area rugs covered the stained hardwood floor, while a motley assortment of freight boxes and a metal folding chair passed for furniture. Kit cringed at the sad clues around her. "Do you live here?"

"Shh." Henry pressed a finger to his lips and smiled. "She'll be home soon. It's a surprise."

"So you said." Kit frowned as Henry puttered about the room, straightening what little there was. "Didn't you spend last night at the shelter?"

He tossed her a ratty pillow that he'd probably fished out of a Dumpster. "Have a seat." She'd pass. "Can I get you a drink?"

"Henry!" The old man's life flashed before her eyes when she saw what he was using for a cabinet. He'd stuck his hand inside a cubbyhole in the wall—right next to a metal conduit that ran from ceiling to floor. Unlike the loose wires protruding from the bare wall frames, this tube looked shiny and new, and probably carried a live current from the lower levels of the building up to the penthouse area at the top. It reminded her of that contraption she'd found in the utility closet at the hospital last night. It reminded her that one man—a supposed expert—had already been killed by a jolt of electricity here at the Sinclair. "Careful. That could be dangerous."

Though he froze at her warning and let her gently pull him back to the center of the room, she hadn't stopped him from retrieving the whiskey.

She could well imagine that that bottle was where her ten-dollar cab fare from last night had gone. She waved aside the offer of a drink and grimaced as he poured himself a hefty serving in a dirty glass she recognized from the diner. "Henry, I thought Tariq took you to the shelter last night."

"I've been out of town on business." Was that a yes? Whether it was age or the drink talking, the man made no sense. "But I've got the place all fixed up for Janice now."

"Your wife?" The one who'd passed away more than a decade ago?

"Have you seen her? Here." He pulled a cracked black-and-white photograph from his otherwise empty wallet and showed it to her. "Isn't she pretty?"

It was almost impossible to recognize Henry from the old photo that must have been taken on his wedding day. But there was no mistaking the love he had for the woman in the picture. Her image had been touched or caressed so many times over the years that her face had nearly disappeared. Still, Kit handed back the picture and agreed. "She's lovely."

He drained half his glass, wiped the dribble off his chin, then licked his hand. "We lived here when we were first married. She'll be so pleased to know I found us a place here again."

Did she tell him this was an unoccupiable apartment or that his wife was dead? "I thought the Sinclair Tower used to be a bank building."

"Sinclair?" That confused him for a moment. His eyes focused on some distant point in the past. He swallowed the last of his whiskey, but that didn't seem to help. He glanced at Kit as though seeing her for the first time. "Would you care for a drink? Janice wouldn't like it if I didn't offer."

Kit blinked back the tears that burned her eyes. "Henry. It's me, Kit Snow." She pried the bottle from his unresisting fingers and set it out of sight behind a box. "From the diner?" She caught his outstretched fingers in a gentle grip. "You can't stay here. It isn't safe."

"But I told Janice to meet me…"

Kit gave a gentle tug toward the door. "I fixed you coffee and a sandwich for dinner last night. Right downstairs. Remember? Then Tariq drove you to the shelter. You didn't leave town."

Henry followed a couple of steps. "I need a drink." He halted and shook his head. "We'll spoil the surprise."

"Henry." Kit coaxed him forward another step. "You don't live here. You can't stay—"

"No." His gentle features transformed. "No!"

He jerked his hand away, wrenching her sore shoulder. "Ow!"

"Leave before you ruin everything!"

"Henry!" Kit caught her heel on the edge of a rug and tripped as she dodged his flailing arms.

But she never hit the floor. The door swung open behind her. Two hands caught her—one at her elbow, the other at her waist—and set her on her feet. Before the rush of air and strength of hands clearly registered, she was whisked behind a wall of black sweater and broad shoulders.

"Get out."

She knew that growl. The stranger from the hospital. "Where did *you* come from?"

But his terse command left no room for acknowledgment or greeting. Mr. Mysterious was already advancing on poor Henry. "There are laws against trespassing."

Kit tried to circle around him. "I can explain."

But she hit the blockade of his black-clad forearm, and he tucked her behind him again. In the same sweep of motion, he wrapped his hand around Henry's tricep and dragged him out the door. "You need to leave, old-timer."

Henry tucked his chin to his chest and cowered away. He was no match for the taller, bigger man. "Janice will be looking for me."

"You're expecting company?"

"His late wife." Kit raced down the hall behind them. "What are you, some kind of vigilante? Let him go."

"I don't know how you got past Kronemeyer's men." Even without the cloak of night or the leather coat flowing out like a cape behind him, there was something dark and menacing about this man. The length of his stride. The intensity of his purpose. The ragged, seen-it-all rasp in his voice.

"This is complicated to explain, but you need to let him go," Kit enunciated, as though she hadn't made it clear that Henry was no threat. "I know him."

"Doesn't excuse—"

"Stop it. You're hurting him." She pulled at his arm, but the coiled muscles wouldn't budge. Mr. Tall, Dark and Temperamental shrugged her off and pulled a cell phone from his jeans.

When he cocked his head at an acute angle to punch in a number, it drew Kit's attention up to the thin black strap that circled the back of his head. But it wasn't the strap that surprised her. She'd had a sense that everything about him was dark. But the hazy wash of sunlight filtering through the windows at each end of the hall caught and shimmered in a short crop of silvery-gold hair.

"Easting." He spoke into the phone now, expecting whomever was on the other end to snap to. He was half supporting Henry now as he turned into the cut-through that led to a bank of elevators. "I want to rout this building of squatters. I don't want any lawsuits if one of them tumbles down the stairs or a ceiling caves in on them. Yes, today."

Easting? Easting Davitz? Kit hurried after them, forcing aside her curiosity about Tall, *Blond* and Testy, to plead once more for a patience and understanding he didn't seem to possess. "You can't put Henry out on the streets. It's freezing outside. He has no coat."

"If the shelters are full, we'll put them up in a hotel." It was an order to the man on the phone, not an explanation to her. "Just get them out."

He shut the phone, jammed it back into his pocket and punched the elevator's call button without ever releasing Henry.

"Thank you. I guess." It was a nice gesture. The

elevator doors opened. Throwing around money didn't always make things right, but it seemed to be this guy's method of apology.

"Get in." He held on to Henry long enough for the old man to find his balance against the railing inside. "You, too, sweetheart."

Kit blocked the door when he turned to go. "That's it? Stuff us in the elevator and walk away? Who are you? How did you find us? I don't want you beating up on my friends."

He stopped, but didn't turn. "The old man's drunk, not hurt."

"He's sick." In the head, in the heart—whatever happened when age and alcohol and loneliness took over.

"He hurt you. I heard you cry out."

"I was already injured from last night."

With that, he finally stopped walking. After a moment's hesitation, he slowly turned, inspecting her from head to toe with a thoroughness that left her wondering if she'd left her blouse unbuttoned. Even from this distance, his perusal allowed Kit a glimpse of forbidding features— from the broken bump of his hawklike nose to the chiseled thrust of his jaw. He looked too cerebral to be a pirate, too wild to be a spy. But with an eye patch, a scar and one piercing blue eye, she got the idea he could play either role convincingly.

"Shoulder?" he asked.

"How…?" Kit clutched at her bruised collarbone, snatching up a fistful of her brown cardigan and instinctively shielding herself from his perceptive gaze.

"Your posture's off," he explained. "You're holding it higher than the other. Favoring it."

About the same moment she realized she was still staring at his unsmiling face, he reached inside the elevator and punched the lobby button. Before she could apologize for her rudeness, he was striding away. "If you need to see a doctor, send me the bill."

"Send it to whom?" The door was closing. He turned the corner and was gone.

Uh-uh. He wasn't vanishing like a puff of smoke in the shadows this time.

Kit hit door open button and gave Henry's hand a gentle squeeze. "I'll meet you downstairs. Germane will be in the diner—just knock on the window and he'll let you in. I'll be down in a minute to get you some coffee to warm you up. We can talk about Janice then."

Mentioning his late wife's name brought a glimmer of life to Henry's stricken expression. He nodded, understanding. "Downstairs. She'll find us there."

Kit slipped out as the door closed. She dashed around the corner and skidded to a halt. No way.

He was gone. Impossible. "You are not superhuman."

But he did smell good.

She inhaled more purposefully this time, and detected a scent in the air that renewed her determination to find him. It was the same stringent scent of soap and skin she remembered from last night. His scent.

Tipping her nose into the air, Kit retraced her steps back to the landing where the stairs and elevators converged. Careful habit had her skirting the dust-framed footprints that had first drawn her onto the thirteenth floor. They were hints that someone had recently been here. She'd hoped one of the smaller prints would belong to Helen's small support shoe—or to a construction worker who might have seen her. Instead, she'd found Henry Phipps. Maybe he wasn't the only homeless person who'd adopted an apartment for himself on one of the Sinclair Tower's unfinished floors.

She followed her would-be rescuer's plain masculine scent through an archway masked with faded drapes that had shredded with age and use. Sniffling at the dust, she lost the smell she'd been following. But her ears wouldn't fail her. Behind the drapes, the sound of sure, striding footsteps led her into a service corridor that ran the length of the hallway on the other side of the wall.

"Hello?" Trusting sound and touch until her eyes could adjust to the deeper shadows of the windowless passage, Kit guided herself along the wall and hurried after him. "Hey! Is money your answer to everything?" Ahead of her, the blank darkness became a black silhouette, the silhouette a silver-haired ghost. Kit quickened her pace to catch him. "I appreciate the change you left me to call a cab last night."

The footfalls ended and she knew he'd stopped. Kit halted a few feet behind him, wondering if it was her relentless pursuit or the dull brass door in front of him that had finally allowed her to catch him. "I know you're Helen's friend. I recognize your voice. It's very…distinct." That was less embarrassing than admitting she recognized him by smell or touch, too. "How is she this morning?"

In the dim light, his expression would be hard to read. If he refused to turn and face her, it would be impossible.

"I didn't come downstairs to chat."

So he lived upstairs. "No, you came down to bully an old man who's dealing with the onset of senility."

His shoulders heaved with a breath that seemed to shrink the space in the corridor down to the few feet that separated them. But he still kept his focus trained on what Kit could now see was an elevator door. "Dr. Osbourn said she was resting quietly this morning. Her functions are normal. But she hasn't awakened yet."

"How did she look?" No answer. "You mean you just called? You didn't go see her?"

"She'll know I was there."

"Yeah, one rose. Big whup." Kit propped her hands at her hips. "She's alone. Apparently, you care about her, but not enough to actually spend some time with her. That's what she needs—your company, not some polite inquiry. You have to talk to her, hold her hand—give her a reason to come back."

"Katherine Snow, right?" His voice crackled with accusatory static.

"Kit. Katherine was for when I was in trouble with my folks." She shifted a step to the side, improving her view from full back to stern profile. "And how come you know my name, but I don't know yours?"

"You ask a lot of questions, Miss…Kit."

"And you sneak around a lot. Wanna tell me why?"

"No."

He pulled a plastic card from his pocket and reached for an electronic keypad on the wall beside the elevator.

This game was ridiculous. Kit reached around him and grabbed his hand, stopping him from swiping the card. "Stop."

But her impatience backfired. At first she thought she imagined the rough lines crisscrossing the back of his hand. But she squinted into the shadows and saw an almost patchwork look to his skin. The scarring mottled the length of his long, surgeon-like fingers as well.

Unusual. Awful. Miraculous that he could have endured such suffering and still have use of that hand.

But it was the sizzle that leaped from his knuckles to her fingertips that imprinted a memory in her brain she wouldn't soon forget. Heat—raw, potent. Chained. But just barely. And not for long.

The heat of passion? Or danger?

Kit curled her fingers into her palm and withdrew a step. She was out of her league with this guy. Way out.

Maybe running after Tall, Blond and Too Much had been a mistake. He didn't listen to reason. He could easily overpower her. She'd told no one where she was going. And she was…hell, she wasn't even sure what section of the building she was in now.

"What do you want from me, Katherine?"

His hushed, ruined voice skittered like a rough caress along her spine, pricking a trail of goose bumps in its wake.

The deliberate use of her full name—for when

she was in trouble—wasn't lost on her, either. Kit retreated another step. "I'm used to having people look me in the eye when I talk to them."

"You've already seen enough. More than you should." He offered her nothing but the jut of his shoulder.

"Are you Helen's grandson? Nephew?" No response. "Boy toy?"

No, of course, he wouldn't laugh.

"I was trying to find out where she lives in the building." Was that her voice, rattling on like a frightened idiot in the darkness? "I thought the hospital and police could use the information. I thought, if there was someone I should notify—"

"I've taken care of that."

"I also wanted to find out if she has a cat or any plants that need taking care of while she's in the hospital."

"She doesn't have a cat. And you didn't come after me because you wanted to know about Helen."

"Maybe not the only reason," she was honest enough to admit. "You're all she has, aren't you?" Kit's tongue felt dry in her mouth. She should stop talking, stop needing answers, stop wondering about this unique, mysterious man. She should go. "At least tell me your name. What if I said that's how I wanted you to repay this perceived debt you think you owe me?"

"I'd say you don't dream big enough."

Kit pressed her lips together, holding back emotions that were too strong to handle in these dark, intimate shadows. Sorrow she hadn't had time to deal with. Guilt over her brother's downward spiral into anger and grief. Fear that she couldn't keep her parents' legacy of family and community alive, or ever create a career and family of her own. "Oh, I've got plenty of dreams. But I've got to take care of reality first."

Maybe there was something in the catch of her voice. Some vibration in the air that let him sense the shiver of lonely need that left her chilled.

Because he turned around.

"Reality—" the secluded corner bathed his face in shadows "—can be a very tricky thing." But there was no mistaking the piercing scrutiny of that deep-blue eye. Or the wary suspicion that colored his raspy voice. "That's all you want? A name?"

Kit hugged her arms around her middle for a warmth she couldn't quite feel. "From you, yes. Solve the riddle for me. Who are you, to know where hidden passageways are in the Sinclair Tower? To have some means to spy on its tenants? To disrupt the power grid at a city hospital and carry a key to secret places like this one? Who are you?"

After an endless silence when she thought he

might—might—reach through the shadows and touch her cheek, he turned away. He swiped the card and stepped into the elevator. As the brass grating closed, he gave her an answer.

"I'm Damon Sinclair."

DAMON SINCLAIR.

As in multimillionaire CEO of Sinclair Pharmaceuticals? No way. The elevator door closed, the light on the keypad blinked off, and Kit was left standing in stunned surprise in the dark.

Kit turned and felt her way along the gritty wall toward the exit.

Damon Sinclair? As in brilliant scientist who'd revolutionized trauma-room medicine with his synthetic-skin and living-tissue-regeneration formulas? The same man who'd disappeared from the face of the planet after his wife's tragic death?

Eighteen months ago, the papers and TV news channels had been filled with stories about the explosion that had destroyed his lab. With the chemicals and fire, no one should have survived. But he had. Five months later his name was in the news again—a grieving widower who'd resigned from life after his wife's suicide. But there were no pictures of him. No one had seen his face. Was he still hospitalized and fighting for his life? Horribly disfigured?

By the time the real news had died down, the

gossip papers had already picked up the rumors. He'd been committed to an asylum himself. He'd bought his own Mediterranean island and had holed up there. He'd gone to Africa with a doctors abroad charity work program and had gotten lost in the jungles.

Damon Sinclair? How could that be?

She'd studied his work in graduate school. Had even earned a fellowship to apply forensic technology to his artificial and living-tissue products—helping to create a databank for law enforcement entities to analyze his work for crime-scene or victim-identification procedures.

He lived here? Upstairs? He'd been here all this time?

Kit was still in a daze of sensory disorientation and emotional shock when she finally emerged from the service corridor. What had she been thinking, chasing after Dr. Dangerous like that? The man was probably nuts. He was most certainly eccentric and showed signs of agoraphobia. Yet she'd cornered him, argued, reprimanded— she'd touched him. All mistakes when it came to self-preservation. He was so far out of her league—professionally, socially, economically… intellectually—that it was laughable to think she'd had the nerve to confront him.

But it was the man who had her all mixed up inside, not the name.

Her reactions to him had been varied, unexpected, overpowering. There'd been an initial rush of sexual awareness that left her feverish. He was so tall, so hardened, so male. Trading words with him made the blood hum through her veins. He was such a complexity of words and actions and mysterious motivations that she was driven to puzzle him out until she felt as enervated as if she'd competed in some glorious game.

And then she'd seen his face and touched his hand and felt…pity. Her heart turned over at the evidence of injuries that would have turned an ordinary man into an invalid. But her mind argued that pity was the last thing a man like Damon Sinclair would want or need.

While her parents' holding hands had been a symbol to her of love and hope, Damon's touch had been a risky, dangerous thing—a touch that awakened things inside her that were, perhaps, better left alone.

And while Kit pondered what *that* impression meant, she pushed aside the drapes that had hidden the alcove for decades. The daylight blinded her for a moment and she caught the faded velvet with her hand, knocking a cloud of dust into her face, stinging her eyes and tickling her sinuses.

Kit felt the resulting sneeze bursting all the way from her toes.

"Who's there?"

Kit jumped at J. T. Kronemeyer's warning shout. From his position near the elevators, she couldn't tell if he was waiting to catch a ride or if he was performing some kind of inspection. "Good grief." With the reassurance of recognition, she lowered her hand from her stuffy nose to her racing heart. "You startled me."

Kronemeyer popped an antacid tablet into his mouth before straightening his hunched shoulders and striding toward her. He crunched and swallowed in one bite, and from the irritation that flared in his dark eyes, she could see how he might need the extra help. "We have laws against trespassing. The thirteenth through twenty-seventh floors of this building are blocked off for a reason."

"But it wasn't." There had been no barricade to warn her from climbing the stairs, no door to keep her from peeking in.

"These floors are off-limits." He made a fist and knocked at the side of the helmet that squashed his thick black hair. "This is a hard-hat area. We can't guarantee your safety."

What was it with the men in her building today?

She pointed to the elevators and apologized. "Didn't mean to worry you. I was on my way out."

Instead of moving aside, he blocked her path. And it wasn't worry that narrowed his eyes. He plucked a cobweb from her sweater. "What were you doing up here?"

Chasing a phantom neighbor, rescuing homeless men.

"I was looking for a friend." She spread her arms wide, indicating the entire floor. "Obviously, she's not here."

"Who were you looking for?"

Kit brushed at the dust and cobwebs still clinging to her clothes and hair. "Helen Hodges. She's a white-haired lady, maybe late seventies, early eighties. Do you know her?"

"She doesn't live on the thirteenth floor."

"I figured that out. But you do know where she lives, don't you?"

Seeing how his expression soured, she thought J.T. needed another antacid to gnaw on. "Why do you want to find her?"

Why couldn't anyone give her a straight answer to her questions? "That's my business."

"Mrs. Hodges is in the hospital."

"I know. I took her." *Mrs.?* "Does that mean there's a Mr. Hodges?" Kit quickly pieced together what Damon had said. *He'd* taken care of everything. *He* took care of Helen Hodges. "Does she live in the penthouse?"

"You can only access the penthouse through a private elevator. And no one but the owner has a key for that."

"That's not what I asked." Though she now knew who had access to the penthouse elevator. Kit pointed to the jumble of footprints overlapping each other on the hallway's tile floor. "I'm clearly not the first person to come up here. When I saw the traffic the floor was getting, I thought I might find her apartment here. Instead, I discovered a homeless man living in one of your abandoned rooms."

This time Kit didn't wait for explanations or goodbyes. She circled around J.T.'s bulky frame and pushed the elevator button. "Is this working now?" A little of her brother's sarcasm filtered into her voice. "There may be others up here, too. I hope you're rounding them up and giving them the same friendly advice about their safety as you've given me."

"You saw someone else up here?"

A glance behind her revealed the construction chief peering down the length of the hallway. The buttons on the elevator weren't lighting up. Maybe she was wasting her time waiting. "I can show you the rooms if you like."

"No!" he answered far too quickly before wrapping his beefy hand around Kit's arm. "No."

Again? What was this, Grab Kit Snow day? "Hey."

He tucked his clipboard beneath his arm and escorted her into the stairwell with as much finesse and patience as Dr. Sinclair had shown with Henry.

"Now I have to walk you down myself to make sure you're safely clear of the danger zone. We could have hot wires, unstable floors, falling debris." He took the steps two at a time, forcing her to double her pace so he wouldn't drag her off her feet. "What if something happened to you? My men aren't even scheduled to begin work on the thirteenth for weeks."

"You were there," she pointed out.

He stopped on the landing between the tenth and ninth floors and planted his chalky breath right in her face. "Don't get smart with me, lady. *I'm* doing my job. You're lucky I'm not calling the cops. Stay off the upper floors."

"I pay good money to live in this building." Kit jerked her arm from his grasp.

He snatched it right back. "Stay *off* the upper floors. It's for your own good."

KIT CHOPPED the red pepper in two, ripped out its seeds and ribs, then sliced it into strips. She turned the strips on her cutting board and chopped them into bite-size pieces. After scooping the bits into a bowl, she pulled another pepper from the counter and attacked it.

Where the hell did J. T. Kronemeyer get off throwing out threats like that? *Stay off the upper floors.* Kit shook her knife in the air and muttered, "Or else."

I mean, who was he really protecting here? The boss up in the penthouse? Himself? Was he that concerned about someone else getting hurt under his command? Or was there something up there *he* had been looking for? Something he didn't want Kit or anyone else to find.

Damon had tried to get her off the thirteenth floor, too. But, mistaken as he was, she'd had a real sense that he believed he was protecting her from Henry. Kronemeyer had just wanted to get rid of her.

A third pepper fell under her knife as Germane pushed open the swinging stainless door. "Is it safe for me to come in?"

Kit grinned. "Don't worry, you're not on my hit list yet."

"Thank God for that. The veggies in this kitchen aren't safe when you get your dander up like that." He flashed a sympathetic smile. "What's eatin' you today?"

"Men."

"Oh. Then I shouldn't tell you there's a man out front who's come to see you? Three-piece suit. Subtle comb-over."

"To see me?" Now what? Oh, God, please have nothing to do with Matt. "Is he a cop?"

"Dressed too nice for that." He arched an

eyebrow in an expression that recommended caution. "I poured him a cup of coffee, but you're the only thing he ordered."

Kit carried her knife to the sink and washed her hands. "And there's no sign of Henry yet?"

"I tell ya, girl. He never showed."

She'd sent him down the elevator two hours ago. The fact he'd gotten lost between the lobby elevator and the diner's interior entrance worried her. "Do you think his talk about his wife is a sign of something serious? Like Alzheimer's?"

Germane waved her toward the door. "I can't answer that. But I'll make a couple of calls to see if I can find him."

"Thanks." Kit cupped his cheek in a grateful gesture. "I won't be long."

Kit took a moment behind the front counter to smooth her apron and scan the diner. It was still a little early for the lunch rush, so only two of the tables were occupied. The stout, balding man, scrolling through images on a small computer screen, sitting in one of the red vinyl booths was easy to spot.

Instead of wondering any longer about what a man in an expensive, tailored suit could want with her, Kit tucked a stray tendril into her ponytail and crossed the restaurant. "You wanted to see me, sir? I'm Kit Snow."

He closed his laptop before scooting out of the

booth and standing with a grace that belied his portly belly. His smile and handshake seemed sincere. "Easting Davitz. Please, have a seat."

Like an old-school gentleman, Easting waited until Kit slid into the opposite seat before resuming his place at the table.

"Davitz, huh? You're the man I send the rent checks to."

He opened his briefcase on the tabletop and replaced the computer before pulling out an envelope. "I'm also chief operating officer at Sinclair Pharmaceuticals. I'm project manager, investment supervisor, executive liaison…and occasional messenger."

"I'm not getting evicted, am I?" Could Kronemeyer have put through a call already and filed a complaint? "You're not closing down the diner so Kronemeyer Construction can sandblast the limestone out front or some other cosmetic thing, are you?" She leaned in. "We do a little better than break even with the restaurant. But I can't afford a shutdown, even a temporary one."

"Relax. No one's closing Snow's Barbecue." He smiled as he wiped the case with a paper napkin before setting it on the floor beside him. "As you may or may not know, Helen Hodges has been a longtime associate of the Sinclair family."

An uncomfortable suspicion replaced the defensive panic of a moment ago. Kit folded her arms across her stomach. Though no one had been eager to tell her anything about Helen, she'd finally been able to piece together that much. "I don't know what her relationship is to the Sinclairs, but I gather she lives in the penthouse upstairs. I meant to get to the hospital this morning, but I got delayed, and then I had to start prepping for lunch." Oh, hell. Just ask. "Has there been a change in her condition? She's not...?"

"Her condition remains unchanged. The doctor says it's like she's asleep. We just need someone to convince her to wake up. But she's still very much alive," he reassured her.

Though she breathed a little easier at the news, Kit frowned. "Then what are you here for?"

He laid the envelope on the center of the table and pushed it toward her. The green-and-white SinPharm logo stood out in bold print at the corner of the envelope. "This is a gift Dr. Sinclair would like you to have, to thank you for risking your life to protect Helen—and for staying at her side when he couldn't be there for her."

You mean, when he chose not to be there.

Kit opened the envelope and pulled out a check written for an obscene amount of money. "Oh, my God."

While she worked her mind around all the zeros, Easting Davitz continued with his spiel. "That should pay your lease in full for ten years.

Since the Sinclair family owns the building and controls the rent, we can guarantee that the price is fixed and that that amount should be sufficient. Of course, if there's something else you need—a new appliance, hiring more staff—"

"I already got what I wanted from Dr. Sinclair." A straight answer. A name to put with the voice and secrets and disturbing fascination.

"You met with him? But I... Where? When?" Mr. Davitz seemed stunned by the news.

If meeting in the dark corner of a hidden corridor and trading hushed, heated whispers counted as a meeting, then yes—it had been a meeting of executive magnitude. But Kit just shrugged. "I've bumped into him a couple of times."

"Really? He didn't mention it."

Apparently, he'd made a far bigger impression on her than she had on him. But then, crusading chemists like her, who spent their time studying and working and taking care of their families, rarely turned a man's head. It had been like that in college, and it was that way here in K.C.

But it wasn't a bruised feminine ego that made Kit stuff the check back into the envelope. "He can keep his money."

Davitz tried another tactic. "Maybe you could apply it toward your brother's education."

"How do you know about my brother?"

"Dr. Sinclair pays me very well to know things."

Kit slid the envelope back across the table. "I am not taking Dr. Sinclair's check."

"Perhaps there's a charity you'd like to donate it to."

"Perhaps you're not getting the message." Had Damon sent his COO with a check before or after she'd made it clear that money couldn't buy the kind of dreams she needed fulfilled? The first option spoke of arrogance, the second of insult. "I would have done what I did for anybody. I want this neighborhood to be a safe place. I want this to feel like a home again. I want my brother to have hope that there's a future for him here. I want to believe that if I were ever in that same situation, that someone would open their door and help me, too."

The bell above the front entrance jingled, alerting her to the six men who walked in. As they hung up their coats and looked to her expectantly for service, Kit expelled a righteous breath and stood. "I'm sorry. These men have a limited lunch break. I have to go."

"Dr. Sinclair will be disappointed that you didn't take the money."

"I'm disappointed that he didn't bring it to me himself. You know, a good neighbor shouldn't be afraid to talk to another good neighbor."

"Dr. Sinclair doesn't take public meetings."

No. He only had the courage to converse from the shadows or dark of night. Or through his checkbook. The infamous Damon Sinclair didn't seem to care much for the real world or its problems—or its people.

She was beginning to like the man in the shadows better than Easting Davitz's cold, absent boss.

"That's his loss."

Chapter Five

"You said he wouldn't come out. He not only left the penthouse, he left the building."

"I underestimated his attachment to that old woman." Though the alcohol would sterilize the questionably clean glasses, one whiskey and soda sitting on top of the box between them remained untouched. "Still, I believe there's a way we can use his new boldness to our advantage."

"How? We've lost any advantage we had. That old woman's seen my face."

"Idiot. She's seen all our faces." How irritating that all this emotional second-guessing could so easily distract a group of colleagues from a perfect, well-thought-out plan. A demonstration of staying cool, calm and collected was in order. "Has she said anything to the police yet? Has she said anything to Dr. Sinclair?"

"Well, no. She's in a coma."

The youngest member of their group suddenly

grinned from ear to ear. "Yo—she doesn't have to stay that way. She's what, like, a hundred? A pillow could fall on her face or something like that, and no one would ever suspect a thing."

"Helen Hodges is seventy-nine." *Older than you'll ever be if you don't learn to control that mouth.* "You stick to your computers and leave the strategy to me."

Leaving the drink behind, the one in charge rose and crossed to the window without touching anything. There had to be a way to make all this still work. A minor setback—a woman who should be dead still clinging to life—would not ruin this.

But the black-haired man who had once been a charming equal was forever impatient. "I haven't seen any return on my investment yet."

"I thought getting me on board was why you paid all that money up-front." The sunset was particularly dull this evening. Probably an indication of more snow on the way. That thought was enough to make bones ache, but not enough to lose focus. "None of this works without an inside man."

"None of this is working, period. You promised me results eighteen months ago."

"Eighteen months ago you trusted the most important part of my plan to an incompetent." A mistake that had been personally rectified and buried deep in the Sinclair Tower's remodeling project. "I've done everything within my power to get us back on our original path. Be patient."

"Patient? I've been with you for two years on this. Where are the millions of dollars that are supposed to be coming my way?" Now the troublesome allies enlisted for the project turned on each other. "If you had taken care of her the way you were supposed to—"

"Me? I do the technical work, man. You're supposed to provide the muscle."

"It's a damn good thing I was there that night to take care of collateral damage, or we'd really be screwed. Now that short-order cook is poking around the Tower like she owns the place. What if she stumbles onto what we're doing? For an abandoned building, there sure is an awful lot of traffic."

"Stop it. Both of you. You're behaving like children." Their panicked bickering intensified a headache that was already debilitating enough. How tempting it was to pull out a gun and shoot. "Katherine Snow has no idea what's going on. We need to focus. We are attempting to outwit one of the smartest men on the planet. We cannot afford any more mistakes." Their technical expert needed to focus on his job, and nothing else. "Are you sure that Helen's key card doesn't work?"

"I tried to get into Sinclair's lab a dozen times

last night and this morning. Either he reprogrammed the cards as soon as the old lady went down, or he's already changed the access codes."

"Codes, codes, codes! I'm tired of hearing that word!" Pounding a fist against the wall only produced plaster dust and a half-dozen splinters. The tense silence that followed secured everyone's full attention and allowed a moment to regather composure. "We should already have that regeneration formula in production. We should already be seeing profits by now."

"He knows what we're doing. The man is on to us."

A smile drove the brainiac punk back a step. "Actually, he knows what *you're* doing. He'll never see *us* coming." The one in charge pulled out a handkerchief and wiped the droplets of blood from the tiny hand wounds. "Run your program again tonight. Maybe we'll get lucky."

"And if he locks me out or changes the passwords again?" He pinched his thumb and forefinger together. "More than once now, he's come that close to backtracking the feed and locking up *my* computer."

"What we need is something to distract Dr. Sinclair."

"Impossible. That man's obsessed with his work."

"Do not underestimate what I can do." *Yes, of*

course. But it would require a delicate touch. "Maybe your idea of an accident at the hospital has merit. Our miscues in the lab have produced some other interesting by-products. Did you bring the samples with you?"

The black-haired man opened one of the boxes and pulled out a small plastic case that held a dozen vials. "We have the 423 and 428 formulas here. Are either of these what you're looking for?"

"The 428 will do. Hand me a syringe."

Though they'd yet to reap the fortune promised by Damon Sinclair's stolen binders, those *miscues* in the translation of his encrypted equations had generated a few useful results. Nothing they could market to the public, but there were military applications that could be pursued. And then there was the whole untapped criminal world that would be interested in paying them a pretty penny.

Success on the black market would be a profitable consolation prize, but not a victory.

"You want me to visit the old lady tonight?"

"No. I'll take care of it." It would be inordinately satisfying to eliminate the excess baggage that had been siphoning retirement funds and benefit gifts from the SinPharm fortune for years.

With a careful precision to detail, the needle slid through the vial's rubber stopper and sucked up the clear yellow liquid. One dose. Two. Three, just in case.

With the syringe loaded, a controlling calm settled in once more. "You—back to your computer. You? Get me into that lab. And you…?" One couldn't help but smile at the drop of miracle potion glittering at the tip of the needle. "Our witness will never wake up."

"*MY* LOSS?" Damon completed three more reps with the hand weights as he listened to Easting's report over the hands-free phone hooked to his ear. "She doesn't have to use the money on herself. She could donate it to a homeless shelter, since she has such a penchant for helping them out."

"I made several alternate suggestions myself." Easting cleared his throat—his way of telling Damon he wouldn't like what he was going to hear. "She threw it back in your face, I'm afraid. Said she'd already gotten what she wanted from you—whatever that means."

A name.

A truth.

How could a woman who owned a rebuilt restaurant, had a brother to put through college and a degree to finish up herself not need a financial cushion? It just didn't make practical sense.

What could she really want from him?

Damon took a seat on the weight bench and worked his legs while Easting continued.

"Apparently, she won't accept any kind of reward unless you present it to her yourself."

"Not gonna happen." He'd already gotten entirely too close to Kit Snow. More than once. Like any faulty experiment, he intended to learn from the mistake. And keep his distance.

"Then she proceeded to give me this lecture about the ills of society. She went on about how she and her brother don't feel as safe in the neighborhood as they used to. It sounded as though she blamed you for it."

"Me?" Damn nervy woman. "Who does she think paid for all the security cameras around the building? The smoke detectors? Does she grasp the idea that I'm making this building more structurally sound, not just aesthetically pleasing? Taking ownership of the building in the first place is a big step toward upgrading the area and bringing in new people and jobs."

"Your arguments are wasted on me, sir." Of course. Easting Davitz had been with the company since Damon's father had first negotiated the start-up money. Almost like family himself, he'd been a part of every major corporate and financial decision, including the purchase and planning development of the Sinclair Tower. Damon trusted they were on the same page with this one. "And don't worry about the homeless fellow. I alerted Kronemeyer to the squatters on the unfinished floors and he assured me he'd get them comfortably settled elsewhere."

Kronemeyer's word was getting to be a questionable reassurance these days. But Easting was clearing his throat again. "What else?"

"Miss Snow suggested that you could be a better neighbor."

The weights clanked together as Damon dropped his legs and sat up. "What?"

"Perhaps she's looking for you to become a patron of the diner. The decor was a little quaint and kitschy for my tastes, but the smells from the kitchen were certainly enticing."

"She wants me to eat her food?" Damon grabbed a towel to mop his chest and back and headed for the shower.

Easting's laughter did little to ease Damon's irritation with the stubborn lady downstairs. "Perhaps we've underestimated her and she's thinking in more corporate terms. An endorsement from the Sinclair family would certainly gain notice in the society page. A word from you or me could guarantee visits from restaurant critics and reviews in the Kansas City papers."

Other than quarterly reports in the business section, the Kansas City papers seemed to have finally forgotten about the *Tortured Husband, Grieving Corporate Magnate, Mad Scientist* who had once ruled the headlines. Wouldn't that be a shock to the movers and shakers and socialites he'd once rubbed elbows with if the brilliant wunderkind of medical miracles showed up at a charity event and told everyone to eat at Snow's Barbecue?

About as big a shock as the face staring back at him from the bathroom mirror. Damon peeled off his eyepatch and stared at the scarred socket and skin he kept hidden beneath it.

The early stages of his tissue regeneration work had been intended for emergency use—a way to close a wound in the middle of a battle-field or temporarily attach a digit that had been severed in an accident or at a work site. Damon's face and hands had healed relatively quickly—miraculously, by typical medical standards. But because of their synthetic molecular base, cosmetic surgery couldn't do much to make it pretty. It was a drawback that he'd refined over the past year. Newer patients to use the treat-ment generated more natural musculature and smoother skin.

Damon's prototype treatments were functional enough. But if he couldn't get used to the shock of seeing himself in the mirror, how could anyone else? Maybe Miranda had been right—outward appearance, whether movie-star gorgeous or Joe Schmoe average—truly affected how the world saw a person. It affected how a person saw herself.

Himself.

With a face and hands like his, how could he ever be...normal?

"Damon? You still there?" Easting's voice in his ear roused him from the painful memories of Miranda's last days. And the pain of his own lonely self-incarceration.

"I'm here. We are not using the Sinclair name to promote Kit...Miss Snow's restaurant. I don't want that kind of publicity." He stripped his sweats and shorts and ran the hot water for his shower. "I'll come up with another way to repay her."

"I'm sure you'll devise something completely appropriate. In the meantime..."

While Easting went through an accounting of business affairs that had been handled throughout the day, and briefed him on upcoming concerns, Damon opened the shower stall to let the steam start permeating both the real and artificial pores in his skin.

The moist heat seeped into his blood and triggered an unbidden memory of those tense minutes in the access corridor with Kit. On a winter's day, in an unheated passageway, he'd felt his temperature rise from the inside out. She'd touched his hand—in protest, in anger—not in passion. But his body had reacted with a lurching, needy response just the same. Things that had been dead for a long time inside him had decided to live again for a few moments that morning. He'd *felt* that touch. He'd felt that contact with another human being in a way he hadn't been able to feel anything for months.

He'd felt *her.*

His good eye had adapted to the shadows so well that he could see the filmy cobweb caught on a tendril of caramel-colored hair. In a rare moment of acting without thinking, he'd very nearly reached out to smooth the lock from her lightly freckled cheek.

But he wasn't a man who surrendered control for long and, wisely, he'd retreated.

Now, though, with Easting droning in his ear and the steam warming every muscle in his body, Damon was thinking again. He was imagining what Kit Snow would look like, washing the cobwebs and dust from her wavy, golden-brown hair. Removing her jeans and sweater and whatever she wore beneath them, and stepping into the shower to wash away the dust and grit.

Damon's memories of a naked woman—of Miranda—were of willowy height and cool, fair skin.

But tonight, as the heat of steam and workout and imagination consumed him, Damon's mind could only picture a curvier, more compact figure. Darker hair, duskier skin. Lots of talk. Plenty of sass. Naked in the shower. Naked in *his* shower. Naked in his shower with *him.*

Mmm. Yeah. For a scientist, he had a pretty fair imagination. But it would be so much more satisfying to explore the facts.

"Damn." He was squeezing the edge of the sink with enough force to snap the porcelain in two.

"Excuse me?"

Mental note: Kit Snow must remain clothed in every single thought.

Damon adjusted the shower to a cooler temperature and made a conscious effort to regain control of his hormones. "I'm sorry, Easting. I got sidetracked on an idea. What were you saying?"

"Something profitable, I hope."

Not likely. "You mentioned Kenichi Labs?"

"Yes. Ken Kenichi is in the country this week. Apparently, they're having some issues getting set up in the new Osaka lab. I've arranged a meeting to go over how SinPharm can supply the extra chemicals they're having trouble importing, but it sounds as though there's a processing issue that requires your scientific input." Easting coughed, and Damon waited for the bad news. "Normally, I'd fax the schematics to the penthouse, but I have some contracts that need your signature, anyway. Plus, I'm having dinner with a friend tonight, so I was hoping…"

Damon nodded at the unasked question. "I'll stop by the office tonight. Leave the paperwork on my desk. I'll look at the schematics and make some notes for Ken."

"At the usual time?"

After all but the skeletal cleaning staff had gone. A handful of people who didn't know to look for him in the first place were easy to get around without being seen.

"Sure. Enjoy your dinner."

Damon disconnected the call and left the phone on his towel. Then he stepped under the bracing fall of water and took the coldest shower he could stand.

After a solitary trip to SinPharm headquarters, he'd swing by the hospital. And, to pay out on some of that give-your-time-not-your-money retribution Kit Snow insisted upon, he'd sit for a while with Helen.

Maybe if he had Helen back in his life, he wouldn't feel this driving need to reach out to his persistent, troublesome, temptingly touchable neighbor downstairs.

"MY FAVORITE IS *The Voyage of the Dawn Treader,* but I thought it made more sense to start at the beginning of the series. The traditional beginning with the Pevensies, even though *The Magician's Nephew* tells how Narnia began."

Kit fingered the worn paperback with a loving caress. A small circle of lamplight illuminated the book in her lap and the wan, peaceful face of the white-haired woman on the pillow. But Kit had traveled miles away from Truman Medical Center's ICU room. She'd traveled back in time to the sound of her mother's voice, reading through the seven *Chronicles of Narnia* during those terrible two weeks in the fifth grade when she'd been home from school fighting pneumonia.

She still felt the comfort of that loving connection which transcended years and growing up and even death. It seemed appropriate now to try to reach out to Helen in the same way, to give her a friendly voice and comforting touch for her mind to cling to while her body healed.

Closing the book with a tender reverence, Kit continued her quiet, one-sided conversation. "This set of books is one of the few things I still have of my mother's. When I went off to college, I didn't have room to haul a bunch of sentimental stuff. But I took these because they always reminded me of Mom and home. And love. Everything I left at home we lost in the fire. But I have these."

An unexpected tear gathered in the corner of her eye, but Kit wiped it away. Helen didn't want to hear sad stories.

"I'll come back tomorrow and read the next two or three chapters to you if you like." When Kit paused for an imagined answer, Helen's soft, even breathing was the only sound in the room. "My brother, Matt, never did get into the Chronicles too much. He's more of a sci-fi nut. Anything that involves starships and aliens and phaser battles. Well, you know boys."

Didn't she? Though detailed facts were hard to come by in her personal investigation of Damon Sinclair, intuition and common sense were beginning to make a plausible version of the truth fall into place. "I'll bet you were around Damon when he was a boy. Before he became *Doctor* Sinclair. He must have liked books, to wind up being as smart as he is. What was he into? Fantasy? Sci-fi? Mysteries? Please don't tell me that the only things he read were textbooks." Kit leaned forward, sharing a conspiratorial whisper. "He wasn't a really nerdy kid, was he? I mean, he went outside and played kickball, shot hoops, tossed water balloons and stuff like that, right?"

Of course there was no answer. Then Kit got the idea to ask something totally off the wall. "Does he have any unusual birthmarks? Tattoos? Piercings? I know that doesn't fit the upper-crust image, but sometimes, with those intellectual types, you never know how they're going to express themselves."

Kit waited a moment, as though Helen might laugh and whisper an answer. "I know. He's too serious for anything like that, isn't he." Feeling an inexplicable disappointment that Damon Sinclair probably was too dour and moody to have any kind of fun streak, Kit slumped back in her chair.

"Well, Helen, I've enjoyed our time together." She set the book on a shelf next to the vase where someone had put Damon's rose in water. Then she stood and stretched the kinks from her muscles. Her shoulder was stiff, though not quite as achy as it had been earlier in the day. "Speaking of the men in our lives, I'd better get home. I was proud of Matt today. He was at work on time and stayed until closing. He was even in a pleasant mood. But I'm a little worried that he chucked his homework and snuck out the door about as soon as I left to see you. I need to make sure he's okay." Feeling an inexplicable connection to the woman, Kit was reluctant to leave. "You raised a teenager. Is this just a phase Matt's going through? I mean, once he learns to deal with Mom and Dad's deaths, I'll get the brother I love back, right?"

Man, she wished Helen really could answer that one.

"Well, good night."

Kit's quilted coat was still damp from the snow that had been falling outside since dinnertime, but her gloves and scarf had dried. She zipped on the coat and stuffed the accessories into her pockets. She had on enough layers to stay warm and dry while she ran outside to her car and scraped the snow off the windshield.

Before donning her gloves, she squeezed Helen's hand one last time. "I'll see you tomorrow."

When the nurse's silhouette filled the doorway behind her, Kit had her excuse ready. "I know, I know. Visiting hours are over." She held her wrist beneath the light and checked the time. "Oh. I didn't realize they'd ended almost an hour ago. Thanks for letting me stay."

"No problem. Good night."

"'Night." Kit was smiling as the door closed softly behind her. That was a different nurse from the plump battle-ax who'd chased her out last night. This one had enough compassion to bend the rules, and Kit was grateful.

She bundled up as she waited for the elevator to arrive. But once she'd pulled her hat over her head and tied her scarf around her neck, Kit realized her hands were empty.

"Oh, fudge." She'd left her book back in Helen's room.

The elevator dinged behind her as Kit spun around and hurried back to the ICU area. The nurse had already turned out Helen's lamp and left, but Kit figured she could duck in and out without incurring any more of the staff's protective wrath.

"Sorry to bother you again." She picked up her book. "Not that I don't trust you. But I didn't want anyone to throw this away by mistake." She pulled off her glove and reached for Helen's hand one more time. "You know how important this—"

A sick feeling shut Kit's mouth and traveled down her throat deep into her gut. "Helen?"

The bony fingers were colder than before.

Kit glanced at the monitors. Everything was still beeping, still registering vital data. She pressed her knuckles to Helen's forehead. It wasn't a freak of circulation. The clammy skin there was just as cold.

"Helen?" She snatched up the call button from on top of the blanket and squeezed it. Again and again. "Come on. This is an emergency." Kit stretched toward the door and tried to summon the nurse the old-fashioned way. "In here! We need help!"

As she pulled another inch, the call-button cord rolled off the blanket and plopped to the floor. "Oh, damn." She quickly snatched it up and cursed. It wasn't plugged in to anything! She flipped on the lamp and saw the empty socket behind the bed. "How long has this been disconnected?"

The monitor cords weren't attached to Helen, either. Instead, they were running off a small black box under Helen's pillow. A box reminiscent of the timing device she'd suspected Damon of using when he'd caused the blackout. "What is going on?"

But the lemonade color of the liquid dripping through Helen's IV tube was the thing that spurred Kit to action. "That was clear a minute ago." Trusting her gut as much as the logical observation that something in Helen's room had gone very wrong, very quickly, Kit took Helen's hand and plucked the tube off the IV needle. The slick, viscous liquid spilled onto Kit's fingers, burning almost the instant it made contact. Cursing at the unexpected sting, Kit wiped it on her jeans and turned for the door. "Hang on. I'm getting the nurse."

Kit had barely taken a step when a blur of blue charged out of the shadows and shoved her across the room. She hit the chair with her knees and toppled, crashing into equipment, knocking over the lamp. But Kit twisted as she fell, landing on her back with her legs free to kick the chair into her attacker.

The escaping shadow tripped, swore, rose from the corner quicker than Kit could scramble to her own feet.

There wasn't even time to shout for help before the tall figure lunged and crashed down on top of Kit. They rolled into the metal bed, knocking it out of place.

She kicked and punched, but her aching shoulder robbed her of strength. A blow to her stomach took away her breath. She tried to catch a glimpse of the man's face. His hair color. Anything. But the figure that struck from the shadows had no face.

Something shiny and sharp glinted in the light from the fallen lamp. Kit caught the descending wrist between her fists and strained, pushed, prayed to keep the weapon from plunging down into her. But her attacker possessed a wild fury Kit couldn't match.

A hand moved to her throat, pressing down on her windpipe with a power that grew as Kit's own resistance waned.

The instant she relented, the fist came down and Kit felt a sharp prick in her arm. "Ow."

Her assailant rolled off her and Kit struggled to sit up and lean against the side of the bed. She was more aware of Helen's limp hand hanging down beside her than of the tall figure retreating into the shadows.

"I'm sorry, Helen. So sor—" Her lungs wheezed with a painful constriction and her shallow, labored breathing became a cough that wrenched through her battered body.

Kit's thick coat had cushioned the crashes and bumps of the fight, but whatever had been injected into her crept through her muscles like clawing, scratching hands, searching for something vital to attack.

Within seconds the room was spinning around

her in a rainbow of dizzying, psychedelic colors. Her muscles softened like gelatin and she sank to the floor.

Her attacker righted the equipment, tucked Helen neatly back beneath the blankets and dragged Kit's boneless body around the foot of the bed, hiding her on the far side of the room.

Kit's head lolled to the side. She couldn't feel her fingers anymore. Couldn't feel the air in her chest. The only thing she could feel was the burning fire seeping through her blood. Through the latticework of gears and lifts beneath the bed, she saw the door open. A pair of feet paused there. "Nurse? Nurse?"

Maybe she only imagined she spoke.

The tall, shapeless shadow closed the door, and Kit's eyelids, heavy as leaden shutters, closed and she knew no more.

Chapter Six

"This is a pretty extreme way to get the neighborhood together for a block party, isn't it?"

Kit blinked her eyes open at the rusty voice in the darkness. Just as slowly they drifted shut again.

Man, that was a heavy sleep. It was hard to feel her body or get her brain kicked into gear. Maybe she was in one of those funky dreams where she only imagined she was waking up.

"Kit?"

"In a minute, Dad."

"Katherine."

That meant trouble.

Party?

"How did you get in my…?" Rusty voice. Not Dad. Wide awake. Danger. Kit got her elbows beneath her and pushed herself up on the bed. "Helen!"

The pitch-dark world swirled around her head,

and a sledgehammer pounded at her temples. Kit clutched at her stomach. Oh, God, she was going to be sick.

"Easy, champ." Strong hands were on her shoulders, gently urging her back onto the pillows. "The acute sensitivity of the senses is normal. But that and the dizziness should wear off in another hour or so."

Yes, she needed to lie down. She needed more sleep.

But the memory of Helen's cold skin, and the strong, angry shadow that wanted her dead, fired adrenaline through Kit's veins. She tugged at the arms that wanted her to rest. "He tried to kill her. Damon, we have to help her."

She had no doubt who belonged to that ruined voice or to the enticingly familiar scents that clung to the shadows. Knowing she wasn't alone should have been a comfort. But Damon Sinclair's presence in the pitch-black room made her too edgy to relax. Maybe it was just the darkness that kept her struggling to sit up and assert her own strength. Maybe it was the knowledge that just because the man was in the room, it didn't mean he was here by choice—or that he had any intention of staying.

"Helen's fine."

"But he was so angry. He'll come back."

"Not tonight. There's a police officer posted at

her door as well as one of my own security men. He won't get to her again. I promise."

Kit's legs tangled in the covers. An IV tube wound around her arm. "Where am I? What time is it?"

"It's 4:00 a.m. I found you just after midnight. I suppose you shamed me into risking another visit to Helen and—"

"Oh, God, 4:00 a.m.? Does my brother know where I am?" Kit tore at the tape holding the needle stuck into the back of her hand. She needed to get out of bed and find a phone. Her brain shifted inside her skull as she swung her legs over the side of the bed and staggered to her feet. "I get on his case about not checking in. And Matty hates hospit—"

Kit was sinking, falling, flying into the dark pit beneath her feet. But she never hit bottom.

Instead, she was captured in a cocoon that smelled deliciously of warm leather. She floated through the air, feeling weightless and warm and infinitely secure.

"Do you go through every moment of your life full steam ahead?" The rusty whisper tickled her ear like the purr of a cat, and Kit snuggled closer. But the heat went away and the purr became a growl of displeasure. "Stay put for a few more hours. The world can manage without you until morning."

While the sharp words dragged her mind back from its half-conscious illusions, the rangy, pantherlike feline hovering over her took the shape of an all-too-human man.

"No." He was back. The man from the shadows. With the needle. And the hate. "Get away from me."

"Kit."

She wedged her fists between them and tried to fight him off. But her arms were like jelly. "Leave me alone."

"It's Damon. I'm not going to hurt you. Now be still before you hurt yourself. Kit, stop!" She quieted at the sharp order—centered herself on the soft wool and leather clutched in her fists and found her way back to a conscious, coherent world as she listened to the calm voice in the darkness. "I called the number in your billfold and introduced myself to Matt. He'll be here in the morning to take you home."

Was she lying down again? How did that happen? "Is he okay? Did he sound worried?"

"He sounded like a grown man who could take care of himself for one night." Matt Snow? Her brother? Grown man? "He also said *G* was staying with him, whatever that means."

"*G* for Germane." Like a second father. One thing in her life she could count on. Kit finally relaxed. "Matty's in good hands, then." Now she could feel the arms sliding out from behind her shoulders and knees. Pulling up the blanket and tucking her in again. She could also sense that one hand couldn't quite hang on to the blanket with the same surety as the other.

"Do you know who I am?"

He'd held her. Cradled her against his chest. Tightly. Gently. He'd held her close until she knew herself again. Until she knew him.

Kit nodded. "Damon Sinclair. Did you just pick me up off the floor?"

"Second time tonight." His scratchy voice retreated into the darkness. "Do you know where you are?"

"Truman Medical Center?"

"One floor above Helen's room, to be exact." He paused long enough that she turned her head to where she'd last heard him speak. "Do you remember what happened?"

"Do I have to?" Kit sank into the pillows and squeezed her eyes shut. Maybe she could pretend she wasn't surrounded by darkness if she couldn't see it. But the shadows inside her head weren't any more peaceful. Jigsaw-puzzle pieces of memory tried to fall into some kind of logical order, but she could only recall flashes of fear and fighting, ice-cold hands and pure, unfiltered anger. And pain.

Her upper arm pulsated with the memory of the drug burning through her blood. Kit rubbed at the swollen, feverish lump where she'd been injected. It was easier to focus on the least of her problems instead of trying to make sense of everything else. "It itches."

The hands that belonged to that unseen face batted her fingers away and probed the injury. "That's normal for an allergic reaction. I suspect that's why you're still alive. Your body fought like hell to reject the drug." He pulled the sleeve of her hospital gown back into place. "Unfortunately, it's also having a hard time processing the antidote I gave you."

"Antidote? What's wrong with me? Did you give Helen the antidote, too?"

"Didn't need to. Your quick thinking saved her before any of the paralytic compound got into her bloodstream."

"Paralytic compound?" Kit could echo the words, but understanding wouldn't come. She felt as though she was in one of her graduate biology classes—only, she'd studied the wrong lesson the night before, and the professor wasn't making much sense.

"No more talking. You need your rest." She heard footsteps crossing the room and knew he was leaving. "I've posted security outside your door, as well. You can throw my money back in my face, but you *won't* say no to my protection. My man's been instructed to stay the night and escort you and your brother home in the morning when you're released."

"Wait. Damon." She reached out into the darkness, needing a hand to hold on to. She needed the reassuring touch of another human being. Needed to know she wasn't alone. "Please. Stay with me."

Her ragged plea hung in the silence. For an endless moment, she half believed that the mysterious Dr. Sinclair had been swallowed up by the very shadows from which he'd appeared.

His answering sigh was measured and deep and chased by an inaudible curse.

Hope fluttered in her chest as she heard him approach. Her pulse quickened in anticipation of the electric contact that had hummed between them yesterday in that hidden corridor.

This time when he touched her, she wouldn't be afraid. She wouldn't be unconscious or delirious, either. She wanted to feel that sizzling pull of curious attraction that made her heart beat stronger—that refilled the well of emotional stamina that had been tapped out.

But he ignored her outstretched fingers, captured her wrist and poked it back beneath the covers. He pulled the blanket up to her chin and smoothed it along either side of her from shoulder to knee. It was an embarrassing rejection that left her feeling more like a swaddled infant than a grown woman who was drawn to the strength of the man in the room with her.

"If you rest quietly, I'll stay for a minute."

Meager as it was, she'd take the offer. "Who is Helen to you?"

"My housekeeper."

"She's more than that."

Damon's heavy sigh stirred the air. She heard him circling the bed. "She's also my former governess. My mother died of cancer when I was young, and Helen was there to fill the role. She kept house for my father, who never remarried. Then she ran the household for me. Now that she's retired I keep her around because she bakes my favorite cookies."

Even in his perpetually gruff tone, she could hear the truth. "You keep her around because you love her."

"I love her oatmeal chocolate chip cookies."

Couldn't he say the words? She opened her eyes, mistakenly thinking she could read some kind of affection in his expression. "Would it kill you to turn on a light? I feel I can hardly breathe, it's so dark in here."

"The degree or absence of light has no bearing on your respiratory system."

Logical bastard. "No, but it affects my mental state. And unless I can get this panicked feeling under control…"

"You? Panic?" Was that a compliment? Or teasing? Intriguing as it might be, the rasp in his tone made it difficult to distinguish any nuances of meaning. But then she heard the supple whisper of leather moving. The lamp beside her bed blazed on, allowing her a millisecond glimpse of a strong, marbled hand before the brightness of the light seared through her retinas and into her brain, forcing her to turn away.

Kit groaned. "Your bedside manner needs some serious work."

"I should have warned you about that." He flipped a towel over the top of the light, muting it and easing the strain on her eyes. "Better?"

Kit nodded, breathing easier as the pain passed. She rolled back to a supine position on the bed and rubbed at her aching skull. "Warned me about what?"

"The side effects of the drug you were given. If it's the stimulant I suspect, it targeted your nerves and left them oversensitized. But the effects should wear off by morning."

"What you suspect?" Though Kit squinted to bring him into focus, he pulled the chair away from the bed and sat. Between the glow of the lamp and the shadows beyond, his face was rendered invisible to her. But his long legs, clad in black jeans and crossed at the ankles, bisected the circle of light and extended beneath her bed, reminding her that Damon Sinclair was a very real man—not just shadows and scent and fevered imagination. "Do you think you could give me an answer in plain English? There's a lot to process right now, and my brain doesn't seem to be cooperating."

"I believe you were injected with an experimental drug that attacks the nervous system and commands it to perform a specific function. In your case, to tell specific parts of your body—muscles, heart, lungs and so on—to go to sleep."

Like euthanizing a pet. Though from her perspective, there didn't seem to be anything merciful about dying that way. "So why didn't it kill me?"

"Something in your body seemed to reject, even reverse the effects. Of course, I'd have to study your bloodwork further to verify my suspicions, but—"

"You studied my blood?" He wouldn't hold her hand, but he had no problem manhandling her in a blackout or playing with her corpuscles? "That's either very intimate or very disturbing."

"I wouldn't have given you anything if I hadn't verified what I was treating first." She'd go with *disturbing*. The man was too damn clinical to feel any sort of compassion.

"What's the purpose of a drug like that? Manipulating nerves and normal body functions? I mean, who would create something like that?"

"I would."

A DOZEN QUESTIONS bubbled up in Kit's throat. *Why would you make such a poison? How do you know its effects will wear off? Have your drugs killed anyone else? Is that why you hole up in your penthouse? How can I be attracted to such a serious head case like you?*

Just what kind of crazy doctor are you, anyway?

But a soft knock at the door intruded and she never got the chance to ask them.

A male nurse cracked the door open and stuck his head in to announce that a pair of detectives from KCPD were outside, waiting to ask Kit some questions of their own.

Kit shrank to the far side of her bed. A glimmer of recognition tried to connect with one of the jumbled impressions she had of the attack in Helen's room. This nurse was as tall as she remembered. His shoulders were broader, but that could be a skewed memory of them charging toward her out of the darkness. This nurse, waiting patiently in the ribbon of light shining from the hallway, seemed genial enough. Good-looking in a boyish way. His black hair was mussed, spiking out in haphazard directions as though he'd just woken up from a nap.

Or had quickly changed his clothes.

Kit squirmed beneath her covers. It was hard to catch a deep breath.

The man who'd attacked her had tackled her. He'd had her pinned before she could really get a good sense of what he looked like.

Hell, she had no idea if that man had been old or young, brunet or blond.

She only knew that an uncomfortable sense of familiarity had her breathing harder and clutching at the metal railing on the bed.

"Miss Snow?" The young man cocked an eyebrow, waiting.

Blue. Hospital scrubs. Her attacker wore blue. That was what seemed familiar.

Kit stilled. "Do all the nurses dress like you?"

He shrugged at the odd question. "Some departments have individual color coding, but it's a pretty standard uniform at Truman."

"Who wears blue?"

"Most of the nursing staff. ICU. Long-term care. Maternity wears pink. That's one reason I'm not working there." He grinned at the notion and excused himself. "I'll let the detectives know you're awake."

"What was that about?"

Kit jumped inside her skin. That voice. She'd forgotten. She wasn't alone.

"Something about him seemed familiar. It's probably…" Kit turned her head. He'd slipped into the shadows again. "…nothing."

Detectives Velasquez and Means could have been interchangeable if not for their ethnic differences in coloring. They were both in their forties, both pushing the heavy side of being fit, both losing a battle with receding hairlines. And both Ric Velasquez and David Means seemed to be at the weary end of a long double shift.

Detective Means scratched at his blond beard stubble and asked her to clarify her description of her attacker. "Can you even tell us if it was a man or woman?"

Kit closed her eyes and tried to concentrate, but the memories weren't there. She shook her head as she opened her eyes. "The last face I remember clearly is the blond nurse who came in to check on Helen as I was leaving."

"Before you returned to get your book? And this guy was already in the room?"

Kit nodded. "I couldn't see his face. It's like it wasn't there."

"Your attacker had no face?"

"I know that doesn't make sense." She couldn't help but let her gaze slide over to the shadowed side of the room where she knew Damon was waiting. As a man who didn't like to show his face, would he qualify as a suspect in KCPD's book?

Damon held himself so perfectly still, breathed so quietly, that she wondered if the two detectives had even sensed his presence. Velasquez's gaze was searching for something, but if Damon didn't want to be a part of this interrogation, then she wouldn't give him away. She waited for Means to stop scribbling in his notebook before going on. "I do know he wore blue scrub pants and hospital shoes. You know, the ones with the cloth bags over them? Like they wear in surgery to protect their shoes."

Detective Means started writing again. "So you think your attacker was a surgical nurse?"

No. The man wasn't getting the details. "I said he was *dressed* like a surgical nurse."

"That describes most of the staff in this hospital," Velasquez suggested. "We could run background checks. Get some work IDs for Miss Snow to look at."

Means countered. "We need to find out how easy it is for someone to get his hands on one of those surgical outfits."

"I can get a list of laundry companies and supply stores."

"That grows our access list exponentially, Ric."

"Maybe Miss Snow can narrow our search with

a more accurate description of the man who gave her that shot."

The detectives' banter ended abruptly. Both turned and nailed Kit with an expectant look.

Her grip on the bed rail tightened.

"Tell us what your attacker looked like one more time." Detective Means held his pen at the ready.

If Kit ever got back to grad school and found the job she'd wanted in forensic science, she knew she'd have to deal with curt police officers who had their emotions turned off and their doubts cranked up like these two. But as a witness with a fuzzy memory and throbbing headache, facing off against their repetitive questions made her feel as though *she* were the clue underneath the microscope.

"I don't remember." Maybe if she sat up, she wouldn't feel like the two men were standing over her, passing judgment and determining she was just as useless to their investigation as Helen's inability to testify was. But moving made her world spin. Though her stomach protested, she propped herself on one elbow and tried to pull out one useful thought. "He was tall. Maybe on the lanky side. But he was so strong. I fought him off for a while. But then…" She surrendered to the pillows again, squeezing her eyes shut. "There was something about his hands. They seemed small for a man."

Kit raked her fingers into her hair, rubbing her palms against her temples. "No. I'm sorry. That's probably just the memory of Helen's hand hanging off the edge of her bed."

Everything was getting mixed up in her head. Kit dragged her hand down to her throat, hating this feeling of incompetence. "He never said anything. He was just so…so…"

"So your attacker didn't have small hands?" Detective Means tried to clarify what she could not.

"I don't know."

"I understand you're a little upset. But are there any details you are sure of?"

She was sure the hand that had choked her into nearly passing out had had plenty of strength behind it. "He wore blue hospital—"

"She's answered enough questions for now." Damon's voice crackled from the shadows. Its unmistakable warning startled her from her turbulent thoughts.

But not half so much as his warm, mottled hand wrapping around her own surprised her. His long surgeon's fingers reached out to her from the darkness. He pulled her fingers from her throat and linked them together with his own in a sure, possessive grip. "She has bruises forming on her neck," he observed, never loosing his hold on her. "You could take a measurement to get an accurate idea of the man's hand size. But do it tomorrow."

With the image of his square jaw outlined above her, Kit closed her eyes again, but only to savor the warmth and courage that radiated from Damon's fingers to hers. She breathed easier now, and the world stopped spinning inside her head. She wasn't alone. And the strength of the man allying himself with her reminded her of the depth of her own strength.

A moment or two passed in silence, and she truly began to understand why her parents had found such comfort, such hope, in this simple act. This was more than a show of support, more than a physical caress. When she felt the rough pad of Damon's thumb brush gently along the length of her fingers, her heart skipped a beat, then calmed and regulated itself at a healthier tempo.

There was an intimacy to be discovered in this palm-to-palm contact. Interlaced fingers were symbolic of other tangled connections that were forming far too quickly and more deeply inside her than she'd ever expected.

"Are you the boyfriend?"

Kit's eyes snapped open at Detective Means's query. Her idyllic bubble burst.

"I'm the doctor. My patient needs her rest."

Means and Velasquez faced off against Damon,

with Kit lying like a prize between them. Detective Means tucked his pen and pad inside his overcoat and pulled out a business card. In the dim glow from the muted lamp, Kit could see Damon from the detectives' suspicious point of view. Dressed in black from head to toe. Eyepatch. Harsh, unsmiling face.

Possessive grip on her.

"Sure, Doctor." Try spy. Kidnapper. Terrorist. "Here's my card. If she thinks of anything else, let us know."

Detective Means extended his right arm, asking for a friendly handshake. Asking Damon to release her.

He did. But only to pluck the card from Means's outstretched hand before tucking Kit back beneath the blanket.

Means couldn't miss the snub. Nor the meshwork of scars on Damon's knuckles. "If we leave now, will you be all right, Miss Snow?"

They suspected Damon? Should she?

But he'd held her hand.

"I'm fine. Dr. Sinclair is…" What? Definitely not the boyfriend. He was neither boy nor friend. "He's my neighbor."

"I see." She had a feeling neither Means nor Velasquez understood her weird connection to Damon. Especially when she didn't understand it herself.

After leaving a second card for her on the bedside table, the detectives left. Damon circled the foot of the bed and followed them to the door. He briefly exchanged words with someone in the hallway before letting the door drift shut.

Half a room away, Kit could feel Damon's energy radiating in waves off his body. Was that the pain of being disfigured? Anger at being pre-judged? He *was* a bit scary to look at in the light. Okay, maybe more than a bit scary.

If she'd ever felt lonely in her life—grieving over the sudden loss of her parents, at her wits' end raising a teenage brother, taking a stand against the crime in her neighborhood—she knew she could only have an inkling of the isolation that Damon must feel. Separated from others by wealth and security and a fearsome face, he was every bit a modern Beast, ostracized from society by their hurtful ignorance or his own protective armor—or some prejudicial combination of both.

Kit's heart squeezed tight in her chest. "I'm sure they don't think you hurt me or Helen. They were just doing their jobs."

Or maybe the man didn't feel anything at all.

"And I'm going to do mine."

"What does that mean?"

"My man's just outside. No one will get in here except your brother and ID'd hospital staff. He'll see you home in the morning. You should be fine once your body has recovered from the shock of the 428 formula."

"Four two eight?"

"You'll be contacted if I find out there are any other aftereffects you should be concerned with."

"Damon. Damon?"

But he was gone. Taking thoughts of compassion and feelings of hope and something too new and confusing to identify with him.

HIS ENEMIES had returned.

Damon wasn't one to completely trust his instincts, but he would soon find the facts to prove what he suspected to be true.

He'd already read the preliminary toxicology reports the hospital had run on Kit and the yellow compound that had been injected into her and into Helen's IV tube. In an old woman, the resulting symptoms would have played out like a heart attack and massive organ failure. No one would have questioned her death. Only a medical examiner who knew what to look for would have discovered any foul play during an autopsy.

But in a vibrant, healthy woman Kit's age…

There could be no other interpretation but cold-blooded murder.

Who would risk such an attack?

The *why* was easier to hypothesize. Someone wanted his attention.

They had it.

Though he had no doubt Kit had gotten in the way of the attempt on Helen's life, he knew a scarf around her windpipe or a blow to the head could have stopped her just as easily—just as permanently—as that syringe.

But this was personal.

Formula 428 showing up on a tox screen made it personal.

Damon shed his coat and stomped the snow from his boots as he crossed the tiled floor of the Sinclair Building's deserted lobby. Canvas tarps covered the navy-and-white art deco mosaics to protect them from pallets loaded with limestone blocks and stacks of lumber and galvanized ductwork waiting to be installed somewhere in the building. Even the architectural rendering advertising the office and living space available after each stage of the remodel was partially hidden behind a clump of sawhorses and power equipment.

Mental note: Have Easting get on Krone-meyer's ass and get this project done!

But he paid no more attention to the hazards and hiding places in a lobby that should have been completed and cleared two months ago. Damon had work of his own to do. He swiped his key card through the access port to the penthouse elevator and punched in his entry code.

Kit Snow had saved Helen's life. Twice. And

she'd damn near gotten herself killed for her efforts. He knew of only one kind of mugger who went from swinging a lead pipe to high-tech assassin in the span of a couple of nights. The same greedy coward who'd destroyed a woman's life to get his hands on a multimillion-dollar medical breakthrough.

Miranda had paid the price for his work.

Helen had paid.

And now Kit Snow was paying. She was lying in a hospital bed, collateral damage easily cast aside because she stood in the way of what some bastard wanted.

His formulas.

His codes.

His corner on the miracle market.

Damon punched the button for the twenty-eighth floor. The car rocked back and forth as its newly installed cables engaged. Bracing his hand against the rail for balance, he swore at Kronemeyer's incompetence. They'd be calling this place Sinclair's Folly if he couldn't get a contractor in here who could complete the renovations quickly and accurately so he wouldn't have to worry about Helen or Kit or anyone else's safety.

And he *was* worried.

He'd made an irrevocable decision tonight, reaching out to Kit Snow. Holding her in his arms. Taking her hand. Quieting her trembling doubts.

He'd gotten involved. Not just to put off some pushy detective who couldn't see how his nagging questions were fragmenting the memories of an attack that she couldn't yet recall. Not just to guide the physician on duty to the synthetic matrix of the venom injected into Kit so that the proper antidote and treatment could be administered.

He'd made her an unspoken promise.

. Kit Snow might be ballsy enough to reject his generous cash donation, but she was damn well going to accept his protection.

No other woman—no other person—was going to suffer because of him.

The number of scientists on the planet who could develop a formula to resequence human nerves to produce a targeted outcome such as tissue growth or system shutdowns was…well… one.

A handful of pharmaceutical companies, such as SinPharm, Kenichi Corp and RetroDyne, produced tissue generation drugs using the chemical patents he supplied. Their scientists produced *his* formulas.

But there was only one way anyone could have independently synthesized his discarded 428 formula so quickly. Someone had been experimenting with his work. His stolen work. They'd produced a bastardized copy of his formula, and instead of saving lives, it took them.

Damon fingered the sealed test tubes with samples of Kit's blood and tissue that he'd stuffed inside his shirt pocket. He would break down the chemical components in his lab, verify that the formula had come from his stolen books.

Whoever had been hacking into his computer, trying to steal his codes, couldn't have sent a clearer message.

If they couldn't get what they wanted from him, then they'd take whatever else they could. They'd taken his wife. They'd taken his work. They'd tried to take Helen.

And now they were after Kit.

She was an innocent bystander who'd gotten twisted up in his nightmare of a life the night she'd taken her skillet out into the alley and become a better friend to Helen than he'd been over the past several months. He owed her.

As the elevator rattled up to the penthouse floors, Damon considered the woman who'd forced him so far out of his solitary comfort zone. He rubbed his thumb across the tips of his fingers, remembering what her hand felt like in his. Her nails were practically short. Her skin was soft and pliant despite the work she did. Perhaps its supple texture was a clue to the source of her subtle vanilla scent.

As the elevator slowed and jerked to a stop, he remembered how she'd burrowed against him when he'd cradled her in his arms. How she'd clung to him as though holding his hand was some big deal. He'd felt her racing pulse. He'd felt how it had evened out and strengthened beneath his touch.

He remembered how his own pulse had leaped at the contact. How long had it been since he held a woman—even a semiconscious one? How long had it been since he'd felt an almost territorial need to touch, to comfort, to connect?

The elevator opened and he crossed the hall to the double glass doors that led to his lab.

Protecting her was one thing. Touching her was something else. A man of Damon's intellect should have known what a mistake that would be. He'd avoided it earlier, when she'd reached out to him. She was lost, disoriented. He rationalized that his rough hands and face were more likely to frighten rather than comfort her. But it had been a futile attempt at maintaining his emotional clarity and detachment.

Because the instant he'd made skin-to-skin contact with Kit Snow, he'd felt something coursing through him he hadn't felt for months. Testosterone, certainly. It was a natural, documented response when something that was his—even just a caramel-haired neighbor—was threatened.

But there'd been something decidedly nonscientific heating his blood that was much harder to explain.

He'd experienced the same inexplicable rush when he'd accidentally grabbed her breast during their struggle in the ICU lobby, when he'd picked her up to protect her from that homeless man she obviously hadn't needed protecting from, and the sweet, clean scent of her hair had caught in his nose.

He'd felt it when she touched his hand in the secret passageway on the thirteenth floor. How wrong had it been to want to caress that dusting of freckles on her cheek? How foolish was he to even imagine silencing the sass from those pretty pink lips with a kiss? How stupid was he for wanting anything from a woman after what he'd done to Miranda?

Mental note: No more touching Katherine Snow.

Refocusing his mind on the way he could best protect his toffee-haired neighbor, Damon swiped his card. The automatic sensor light came on, and he entered his new code and watched the doors slide open. He was still standing there when they closed again.

"What do we have here, Doc?" Damon leaned in closer, careful not to touch the palm print that smudged the clear glass. "We've had company."

A measured look in either direction told him he was alone in the hallway. And since he'd programmed his key port to automatically reset the code each time a door was opened, he had no fear that some unknown intruder was waiting for him in his lab. Not since the fire would he ever have that kind of trouble again.

But someone had tried to get in. Maybe the handprint was evidence that the intruder had tried to pry open the door manually. Or maybe it was a slap of frustration against the glass. Anyone fit enough could climb the stairs to the twenty-eighth floor and, if he or she possessed the patience of a safecracker, one could break a conventional lock to gain access to the penthouse levels. Helen, Easting Davitz, SinPharm security, J. T. Kronemeyer and a select few from his construction crew had access to the private elevator. But no one could get into his lab. No one.

For comparison, Damon splayed his fingers out. The handprint was smaller than his, and there were no distinct lines—no fingerprints—to trace. That indicated the intruder wore gloves. Either that or…Damon turned over his hand and noted the blank fingertips…he wasn't the only deformed freak out there.

Yeah, right. He'd go with the glove theory.

Curling his fingers into his palm to hide the disgusting alternative, Damon entered the lab. He tossed his coat on a hook, booted up the security monitors and slipped into his white lab uniform.

After a quick scan of the cameras to verify that all of the public areas of the building were clear—other than the road grader rumbling past out front, scooping aside the new snow—Damon referenced the time he'd been gone and scrolled through the recorded footage.

Nothing. Nothing. Nothing. "Hello."

Damon highlighted the image and magnified it on the central monitor—11:30 p.m. Shortly after he'd left to sign papers at SinPharm. On the screen the elevator opened and a bulky, shadowy figure stepped out. He looked from side to side. Yes, he was alone. He could go to work.

"Interesting."

The figure on the screen pulled out a key card. Stolen from Kronemeyer or one of his men? Could it be Kronemeyer or one of his men? Damon couldn't see how a man with that much sawdust in his brain could have an interest in his work, much less have the capacity to plan industrial theft. No, this was the work of somebody much smarter.

Somebody willing to kill a sweet old woman just to get her keys. Somebody who *knew* Helen would have that key card. Somebody who knew Helen.

"Come on, you bastard. Show yourself." The intruder swiped the card. The light came on.

The figure on the monitor was wearing a bulky Kansas City Chiefs parka, with a fur-lined hood pulled up over his head—hiding his face and masking his shape. Most likely startled by the light, the intruder swung around, searching to see if he'd been discovered. Something else caught his attention and he tipped his head, looking straight into the camera. "I'll be damned."

"Your attacker had no face?"

Detective Means's incredulous question echoed in Damon's mind. Damon's intruder was wearing a stocking mask that covered his entire face, leaving nothing but dark eyes showing through. Kit's attacker had probably worn a mask, too. He'd have to ask her if she remembered a color or design that the police could add to their description.

Maybe he'd call Detective Means himself when the sun came up. Maybe he wouldn't. He had an idea that Means and Velasquez were way out of their league on this investigation. If Damon wanted to protect Kit, he'd best get to work on the evidence himself.

After copying the tape of the break-in attempt and sending it to SinPharm's security office, Damon geared up and went to work. Sleep and breakfast were optional now. He prepped Kit's bloodwork for testing, erased his white boards and put on his lab glasses.

Knowledge had always meant power in his world. And he intended to make himself the smartest man in this deadly game.

Chapter Seven

His hands were on fire.

Damon fought off the groggy disorientation that consumed him. He let his rage suffuse him. Give him strength. Numb him to the agony of searing flesh. He clutched his arms to his stomach and doubled over to stifle the flames with his own body.

"Help! Damon! Help me!"

"Miranda?" A pain far more cruel than any physical torture twisted in the pit of his stomach. Oh, no. God, no. "Miranda!"

His wife's screams hurt worse than the scorching agony of the skin blistering on his fingers. Her terror cut deeper than the shrapnel wound on his forehead. He'd gladly give up any medical secret he could devise, but please, please, spare his wife.

"Miranda!" He shouldered aside burning tables, melting plastic and shattered glass, desperately searching through the blinding, roiling smoke. "Miranda! Ans—" He choked on the toxic gases coating his lungs and crumpled to the floor.

"Damon!"

Her screech of desperation drove him on. He crawled through corrosive puddles and ruined work and unknown treachery to find the only thing that truly mattered. "Miranda? Please. Keep talking. I'll find—" Coughing cut like broken glass through his raw throat. The spasms drained his strength and drove him to the floor. But he pulled himself toward her ragged sobs. He had to save her. "I'm coming."

"Damon…" Her voice was fading away. Dying.

He was his wife's last—her only—hope for survival.

He reached the storage closet, tossed aside the stool blocking the door, then yanked it open to find her. To save Miranda.

He found her curled into a ball inside. Only this time, her hair was darker—a rich caramel brown with golden highlights. A troublesome tendril had sprung free of its ponytail to drape across a freckled cheek instead of clear, porcelain skin. And instead of crystal-blue eyes hurling accusations at him, large, pale-gray orbs begged him to reach out to her. To save her.

Not Miranda. Kit.

He had to save Kit.

A chunk of ceiling gave way and crashed to the floor, shooting up a snarling roar of white heat and orange flame between them.

"Damon!" A different voice. Kit's voice. "Please!"

He rolled to the side, sucking in the last breath of oxygen hovering above the floor. He thrust his hands into the flames.

"Kit!"

He had to reach her. Had to hold her. Had to save her.

"Kit!"

Their fingertips brushed, curled together, clung. "C'mon, sweetheart. Hold on." But the fire was so intense. So hot. He pulled. But he felt her slipping away. His useless hands came back empty.

"Damon!"

He plunged in again. But he couldn't find her in the fire. He couldn't hold on to her. "Kit? Kit!"

The alarms went off. The fire closed in. "Kit!"

He couldn't save her. Couldn't save her. Couldn't save—

A repetitive buzzing woke Damon from this new, twisted version of his perennial nightmare.

"Son of a bitch." The tension eased out of him on a deep, controlled exhale, and conscious awareness of his surroundings returned on the next breath. Sunlight leaked between the blinds, indicating it was high in the sky. His stomach rumbled in protest of its twenty-four-hour stint without a decent meal. He was lying facedown on his work station, his cheek feverish against the cool stainless top. His arms were stretched across the table and his hands, those experimental recreations of flesh and sinew, were clinging to the far edge of the table with the same ferocity with which he'd tried to hold on to Kit Snow in his dreams.

Damon popped his grip and sat up.

Cold steel was about all those hands were good for. Holding on to a needy, warm-blooded woman, thinking he could help her, wishing he could have her… Damon shot to his feet and rolled the stool away. Two strides carried him across the room to shut off the timer on his experiment. "Shut up."

Only, it wasn't the timer that was beeping.

Now he remembered. His tests had already turned up a result he didn't want to see. Kit shared the same allergic tendencies that Miranda had exhibited. His tissue regeneration formula—and any apparent derivative—would be a toxic shock to her system, not a miracle cure. If the initial introduction didn't kill her, then her body—after a few bothersome side effects—would simply reject the drug. If she wasn't healthy enough, if she didn't have enough antihistamine in her system to block the absorption, then the formula would mutate her nervous system. Like Miranda, Kit would be susceptible to hormonal imbalances and abnormal cell growth. Who knew what other debilitating or even fatal side effects would have eventually presented themselves if Miranda hadn't taken her life?

The annoying buzz started in again, and Damon cursed. He hadn't recognized the sound at first because he hadn't heard it in months. It was from upstairs in the penthouse. Someone had gotten to the twenty-ninth floor and was ringing his doorbell.

Easting never showed up without calling first. Helen was in the hospital. SinPharm security? Again, he'd get a call. That left J. T. Kronemeyer. And with the mess he'd seen downstairs in the lobby last night, and the slack control of a project that allowed homeless people to occupy uninspected floors of the building, that contractor better not be showing his face at Damon's front door.

Scrubbing his palm across his unshaven jaw, Damon shook off the remnants of his sleep and checked out his visitor on the monitors.

"I'll be damned." Persistence had a name. "Kit Snow."

LEAVING HIS WORK behind him, Damon hurried up the back stairs to the penthouse. He draped his lab coat over a black leather sofa, tossed his goggles onto a chair, dimmed the lights and opened the front door. "How the hell did you get up here?"

Her jerk of surprise should have tempered his annoyance. He didn't appreciate trespassers of any kind. But the teasing expression that slowly curved her pink mouth into a beautiful smile altered the adrenaline charging through him. Now his blood pulsed with something equally potent yet far more dangerous. Attraction. Excitement. Pleasure at seeing her face-to-face.

"Good afternoon to you, too." She thumbed over her shoulder toward the recessed exit behind her. "Freight elevator. Besides your private elevator, it's the only conveyance that runs through every story of the building."

His first impression was that she barely reached his chin. A big mouth and lots of bravado made her seem taller.

His second impression was that her skin was pale beneath the sprinkling of freckles on her cheeks. She still wasn't a hundred percent after last night's attack.

Damon's third impression was that something in the basket she carried smelled damn good, enticing enough that his stomach grumbled a wishful invitation before he could find the will to send her away.

Her gaze dropped to the traitorous growl. "Hungry?"

"I worked late last night. I guess I skipped dinner."

"Breakfast and lunch, too, from the sound of things. Man, are you lucky there's a diner right downstairs. May I come in?"

He was politely standing aside and watching her stroll past before he decided it might be wiser to say no. At least no one could hurt her up here. He wouldn't have to rely on the cameras or a security guard to make sure she was safe. Damon closed the door and pointed her toward the kitchen.

"What's in the basket?" He held back a few steps before following her, consciously putting distance between them.

"A thank-you gift. Well, leftovers, really. But then, the diner has killer leftovers, in my ever so humble opinion. Do you have a plate? Or do you want me to stick it in the fridge? Wow." She paused at the entrance to the granite-and-black kitchen, loaded with every amenity Damon had been able to find to make Helen's life easier. "This is almost as big as our restaurant kitchen. You could feed an army in this place. Helen must love it."

The long black-laminate table could hold twelve, but was only set for two. And often Helen ate there alone while he worked. "She says it's too big."

Kit had spotted the lonely place mats. The

sadness of her sigh was almost embarrassing. But she was smiling as she glanced over her shoulder and carried the basket to the table. "Mom and Dad said the kitchen was always the heart of the home. That's why they opened a barbecue joint instead of something fancy. They wanted folks to feel at home. And come back often. Plates?"

Damon retrieved the necessary accoutrements and joined her at the table. He made a point of sitting at the head of the table, so that the sun streaming in through the windows behind him would cast his face in shadows. He left her place mat at the opposite end. Not the friendliest arrangement, he knew. But considering he hadn't entertained a guest in months, she was lucky he was allowing her to stay at all.

But nothing—not even his cautious, watchful demeanor—seemed to disrupt her chatty mood. "This is Germane's shredded beef sandwich. Usually I make the slaw and roasted-potato salad, but I was a little indisposed this morning."

"How are you feeling?" He decided the doctor in him needed to know.

"A little tired. But otherwise, fine." She served up generous portions. "The apple pie's mine, though. Your guard, Oscar, ate three pieces. I managed to set aside a slice for you before the lunch crowd came in, though. I know it's just diner food, but—"

"It's de-liff-us." Damon chewed around the compliment and swallowed. "What's in this sauce?"

"I'm not sure." She seemed pleased that he was plowing through her food. "That's Germane's secret recipe. He and my dad created it back before I was born. Germane says he plans to leave me the list of ingredients in his will—so I hope I don't find out for a long time."

The pie was damn near as good as anything Helen could bake, too, and he told Kit as much.

"That's high praise, indeed, coming from the oatmeal chocolate-chip expert."

Damon laughed, and the sound seemed to capture her full attention. As those dove-gray eyes squinted to bring him into sharper focus, he lowered his head and polished off his plate.

"Do you mind if we talk?" she asked, allowing him his visual privacy.

Damon shrugged. "I haven't been able to stop you yet."

She laughed for him. "I guess I think out loud a lot. And when I get curious about something, I ask."

He tensed. Curious about what?

"Do you have laryngitis?"

Hiding his relief behind an oversize bite of pie, Damon shook his head. It was a safe enough topic. "I always sound like this." He offered a matter-of-fact explanation without going into detail. "There's scarring on my vocal cords and throat."

"From what?"

Maybe not such a safe topic. "There was a fire in my lab."

"The one that was in the news a couple of years ago? What happened?"

"I don't talk about that night." He watched the skin beneath her freckles blanch at his sharp tone.

Now, there was a conversation stopper.

Or not.

"My parents died in a fire. That same night." He didn't think it was possible for her to sound so lifeless. Defeated. "Two fires in the same building on the same night? I remember the arson investigators worked for months trying to make a connection. But they never did. The causes were different. The Snows and Sinclairs had nothing in common. You and your wife got out. Mom and Dad…"

Suddenly the table between them was much too long. Damon tightened his fist around his fork to control the urge to go to her. What did he think he could do? Hold her hand again? It seemed kind of high schoolish. But right now, holding on to Kit sounded like the most perfect way in the world to ease her sadness. To ease his own.

Probably a damn good thing the table was so long.

"Let it go, Kit." Move on. No talk of fires. No talk of anything that might trigger a personal memory or incite an emotion. He just wanted to keep an eye on her. He wanted his own visual verification that she had recovered from the 428 drug.

Her smile made a mockery of his emotional detachment. "Does it hurt when you talk?"

Faulty reasoning, Doc. This wasn't just about keeping a close watch over his headstrong companion. He was enjoying this verbal sparring match. Enjoying her company. More than he should. "Always with the questions."

"Never with the answers." She nailed his intonation right on, and a laugh rasped at the back of his throat again.

"No, it doesn't hurt."

She rested her elbows on the table and propped her chin in her hands. "I guess you'd never know if you did get laryngitis, then."

"Interesting hypothesis."

Sitting together at his kitchen table in the middle of the afternoon, eating, talking—it felt normal. Special. Certainly not like a doctor and patient sharing a meal. Nor even a protector and his big-hearted neighbor who'd put her life in danger because of his mistakes.

Though Miranda had never been this much of a talker, sitting with Kit reminded him of the late-night or early-morning meals he'd shared with his wife. Back when he thought they'd be together forever, when he believed they could get through any rocky patch. Before he spent too much time in his lab, and she, too much time in her office. Back when he'd hoped they could move beyond being business associates and lovers, and start a family.

This was a secluded moment out of time, unfiltered by his private demons or outside dangers. But it wasn't real. It couldn't last.

Kit's next question proved that. "Did you finish running the tests on me?"

Despite his hunger, his appetite failed him. "Yes."

"Well, don't keep me in suspense. Am I going to live?"

If you stay the hell away from me and my enemies, you might. "Yes."

"Has anyone else died because of your experimental drugs?"

Damon pushed away from table. So this visit was more than just a tasty way to thank him for his help. She was fishing for information, just like he was.

"The SinPharm products I've developed have saved thousands of lives. We've helped doctors mend a lot of broken people."

"You didn't answer my question."

Damon scooped up his plate and carried it to the sink. "There are some with allergic predispositions who can't tolerate the medication."

"Like me."

"Exactly. My tissue regeneration therapy meets FDA standards. No one has died from its proper prescription and use." He turned to emphasize that point, found she had followed right behind him, and quickly turned back to face the sink. "Four two eight is something different. It was a failed experiment."

She moved in beside him to set her plate in the sink. "It seemed to work on me."

"You'd be dead if it had worked the way it was supposed to."

Her fork clattered onto her plate. "I warned you about that bedside manner, Doc."

In another time, in another place in his life, Damon would have wrapped his arms around her and held her until the tension that whitened her knuckles and corded the back of her slender neck eased. But he was who he was. He shouldn't even be standing this close to Kit, side by side, shoulder to shoulder. The nubs of her sunny-yellow top caught in the ribs of his black sweater, creating friction. Triggering unseen sparks. Igniting the fluid warmth that seemed to flow between them.

But she needed reassurance. At the very least, she needed an explanation. And Damon needed…

He didn't move away. "The night my lab burned, I had reams of my work stolen. Most of it consisted of discarded formulas."

"Like 428?" She wasn't moving away, either.

Damon nodded. "Everything I record is encrypted. Apparently, whoever stole those books has managed to decipher some of my work and produce the drug. Or they got lucky."

"You don't strike me as the kind of man who believes in luck."

"Not the good kind." Breathing deeply stirred his arm against hers. He felt her shift. Lean in. Damon squeezed his eye shut, damning that surging flood of heat and desire that had him feeling like a whole man. Wanting like any other man. Why the hell wasn't he doing the smart thing and moving away from her soft fire? "My notes are complicated enough that it would take a team of scientists years to make sense of everything in those books. Even longer before anyone could get any viable formula or see any kind of profit."

"So that thief has come back to get your codes?" Smart lady. "Do you think they're using Helen to force you to turn them over?"

"I would never. Helen wouldn't want me to. But hurting her would be the most efficient way to put me off my game. Since Miranda's suicide, she's the only thing I care about anymore." Maybe not the only thing. Was that his little finger toying with the back of Kit's hand? Why was he so fascinated with the blend of strength and softness there? "Their sick greed cost me my wife. I will not give them the satisfaction of succeeding."

"If they're willing to create and use a poison like 428, then they have to be stopped."

He intended to do just that. "I'm afraid you've gotten in the way of whatever they're planning. They can come after me—they can try. But I won't let them hurt you again. I promise."

Kit's fingers shifted, ever so slightly, and suddenly they were holding hands again. The current thrumming between them sizzled to life in an instant.

But she was offering advice and comfort, not making his unspoken wishes come true. "You shouldn't be fighting them on your own. Have you told the authorities?"

"Like Means and Velasquez?" Those two drones couldn't find where they parked their car, much less track down who was behind the fire, the theft, the computer infiltration, Miranda's death and the attacks on Helen and Kit. No, thanks. He'd handle this his way. "I've alerted my executive liaison and he's put my security staff on alert. No one will break into SinPharm."

"It's not your company I'm worried about. Do you have any idea who's behind the theft?"

Damon's laugh was a bitter sound in his throat.

"Most of the world thinks I'm dead. So I'm guessing it's someone who knows me personally. Someone who knows I'd recognize 428 when I saw it. Someone who wouldn't mind destroying my company in the process."

"Do you have a long list of enemies?"

"So you've picked up on the fact I don't have a lot of friends." Following the most natural of impulses, Damon angled his chin down to let her see that that was a fact of life he accepted. One he preferred.

But he froze at the wide-eyed curiosity in her upturned face. She was looking at him. Only inches away. Dead-on. "I've picked up on the fact you don't go out of your way to make any friends."

Damon extricated his fingers and turned away. "Thanks for the late lunch. You'd better head out. I need to get back to work."

Her hand at the center of his back singed his skin. "You know, I don't mind seeing your face."

"You really should go."

He was surprised at how quickly the warmth of her hand disappeared. Had he really been hoping she wouldn't give up so easily? Fine with him. He didn't want her pity. Touchy-feely time was done. Damon stalked to the table to snatch up her basket and send her on her way. She trailed right behind him. "At least it's not boring to look at. I think the eyepatch makes you look like a swashbuckler."

"Swashbuckler?"

"Maybe international spy. It adds mystery. A sense of daring."

He dropped the basket and spun around to meet her. "This is no storybook face, sweetheart. It doesn't get better-lookin' when I smile."

"Let me see," she challenged, folding her arms beneath her breasts and thrusting them up in a way he shouldn't have noticed. His unblinking glare should have backed her off a step. Instead, she threw up her hands and cursed. "This is ridiculous. You'll stand up to KCPD, a hospital staff and some psycho who wants to steal your work and kill your family—but you're afraid to take me on?"

"There's a difference between fear and consideration. I'm responsible for getting you into this mess, and I'm perfectly willing to do whatever it takes to get you out of it in one piece. You did the same for Helen and I owe you. But that doesn't mean I intend to take advantage of the situation."

"Oh, and forcing me to look at your face is taking advantage?"

"Go home, Kit." He was heading for the door.

But she planted herself in his path. She reached up and framed his jaw between her hands and demanded that he listen. "Don't you feel it? Am I nuts, or is there something going on between us?"

She was touching him. Oh, yeah, he was feeling it. Every cell in his body leaped with traitorous joy. *Wait for the rejection, boys. You've been without a woman for a year and a half now. If you do what you really want, you'll scare the crap out of her.* Damon closed his hands around her wrists to pull her away. "It's probably some sort of rescuer complex. Pity and gratitude are getting all mixed up inside your head."

She tugged herself free but didn't budge. "I don't have a lot of experience with men, Damon, but I think you piss me off too often for me to be feeling pity. And as for gratitude…"

Her tongue stopped on an uncharacteristic stutter. Her whole posture changed, retreated. "Is that what you feel for *me?* Gratitude? Because of Helen?" She studied his chest from shoulder to shoulder for a moment before tipping her chin to look him in the eye again. "I'm not any sort of ally or confidante who shares a common enemy with you, am I? I'm the buttinsky neighbor who gets on your nerves and gets in your way and disrupts your routine." She was backing away now, her mouth lined with bitter apology. "There's no chemistry here, besides your lab and my degree."

"Kit—"

"Let's call it even, okay, Dr. Sinclair? I don't want you putting up with me out of gratitude any more than I want you writing me off with an embarrassingly large check. Thanks for saving my life. Good luck catching the bad guys. Say hi to Helen for me." She darted around him to retrieve her basket from the table. "And I hope you enjoyed lunch."

"Katherine." He snagged her wrist as she hurried past. He cupped her cheek and tunneled his fingers into the fringe of her hair. "It's *not* gratitude."

He damned caution and common sense and lowered his head to kiss her.

Her lips tensed with a startled gasp, then softened beneath his. It was just mouths at first—testing, tasting, parting. She rested a hand on his biceps. He teased the band that tried to control her hair. He traced the seam of her lips with his tongue and she opened for him with a shuddering sigh that caressed his eardrums and danced along his spine.

Kit was every bit as warm and sweet as he had imagined. And she was every bit an equal partner in this kiss as he was.

Her responses were cautious at first, then grew bolder with each foray as he welcomed her curious exploration of his mouth. She found the sensitive arc of his bottom lip. The seam of his dimple. The matching flavor of sweet and tart from their lunch on his tongue.

"*This* is chemistry," she whispered.

"Advanced," he clarified.

It was a damn fool's game as well, but that didn't stop Damon from finding the nip of her waist or settling a possessive hand on the swell of her hip and drawing her back to the table with him. He sat on the edge and pulled her into the vee of his legs, aligning her heat with his own. Easing the strain on her neck. Tempting every eager, aching cell of his chest with the teasing brush of her breasts. He pried the basket from her unresisting fingers and guided her hand back to his face. He wanted to feel her acceptance of him, needed to feel she wasn't afraid.

Of her own volition, Kit lifted her other hand to his jaw. He deepened the kiss and she rose up on tiptoe, meeting him halfway. Damon freed her ponytail and sifted his fingers through the silky waves at the nape of her neck.

Other than a fond peck on Helen's cheek, Damon hadn't kissed a woman in months. He hadn't wanted to. But now, with the blood rushing in his ears and pooling south of his belt buckle, he wondered why he'd waited even two days to kiss this one.

He'd deprived himself of a woman's touch. He'd wallowed in his grief, refused to want. His work was his mistress, retribution his only need.

Damon squeezed Kit's bottom and lifted her more fully against him. She moaned into his mouth at the frictive contact of lips and bodies. He absorbed the sound deep inside, where it opened a fissure in the loneliness and guilt that imprisoned his soul.

Her bold fingers stanched the same wound, running across each ridge and hollow of his face—learning the tragic imprint of his life stamped there. Soothing him. Accepting him. A tickle at the bump of his nose, a scrape against his stubbled chin, a lingering stroke along the line of his jaw.

Then she discovered the strap that anchored his eyepatch in place and the first intrusion of rational thinking snuck in. Damon lowered her to the floor.

She traced the strap to the back of his head and he slid his hands to a less intimate grasp at her waist. She followed the strap back to the leather circle that hid his disfigurement. She fingered the leather and frowned against his mouth. "Is this from the fire, too?"

Reality shot through Damon like an ice-cold lightning bolt.

He pushed at her waist. Pushed her away. Pushed to his feet and turned her toward the living room.

"You and I will talk later. I need to shower and sleep and run some more tests. I should be able to trace the source of the chemicals used to drug you, if not an actual manufacturer's matrix. We might be able to track a purchase or theft if we know where it came from."

"Damon. What's wrong?"

"Don't leave the building without telling me." He thrust the empty basket into her beautiful hands and led her to the door. "Don't leave without Oscar or another SinPharm guard to escort you."

"I won't. But—"

"What just happened here will not happen again. Understood? I need time to think. Time to figure out what's going on before anyone else gets hurt."

The confusion and hurt that darkened her eyes was hard to ignore. "If we put our heads together, we stand a better chance of—"

"I can't keep you safe if I can't think."

"Being alone is not the answer."

"It is for me."

Damon pushed her into the hall and closed the door. He waited on his side, listening to her shocked silence and the well-deserved curse and stomp of footsteps that followed. He didn't move until he heard the ratcheting sound of the freight elevator gate opening and closing.

When he heard the gears cranking against the elevator's descent, he turned and faced the dramatic, two-story layout of his so-called home. The squared-off arches and steel stairs to the bedroom loft were purposeful, masculine touches. He'd stripped the penthouse of every trace of his wife, every trace of the love they'd shared. He changed the decor, changed the pictures, changed the warmth. Miranda was gone.

But he couldn't seem to get the traces of Kit Snow out of his sanctuary. Her scent hung in the air. Her apple pie and bold kisses lingered on his tongue.

"You've got degrees from Mizzou, Johns Hopkins and MIT, and you still can make a stupid mistake like that?" Damon chastised himself and peeled off his clothes, tossing the scent of temptation into the hamper and stepping into the shower to let the coldest water he could stand beat some sense into him. "That was definitely not gratitude."

Not on his part.

"Swashbuckler?" He *was* feeling a little piratical, taking advantage of Kit's curiosity like that. He'd done her a disservice in thinking what she felt for him was pity. But he'd be doing himself a disservice if he was crazy enough to believe that anything beyond her innate scientific inquisitiveness had prompted her to respond to his kiss.

It sure wasn't lust. It wasn't caring. And it wasn't going to happen again.

Not until he hunted down his enemy and made him pay.

After that, there'd be no reason for Kit Snow to barge into his life and mess with his head.

No reason at all.

Chapter Eight

"Aren't you even the least bit concerned that a man who was living in the building where you work hasn't been seen for three days? What if there's been another accident? Your company could be liable."

J. T. Kronemeyer popped an antacid tablet into his mouth before responding to Kit's questions. "Henry Phipps does not live here. The fact that he's labeled homeless indicates that this is not his home. Now can I get my glass of milk?"

Kit didn't know whether to be angry that no one else seemed to be missing Henry, or afraid that he'd wandered off into the frozen night, searching for a wife he would never find. "None of your men have reported seeing him anywhere in the building?"

Kronemeyer gestured to the half-eaten dinner on the table in front of him. "Look, Miss Snow, I'm sorry that I had to get rough with you upstairs the other day. I'm under a lot of pressure to get this job done, and what with chasing out squatters, losing reliable men and having supply orders come in late, I'm getting further behind."

"Have you lost another man?"

"Why do you think I'm staying in town tonight? I have to go back to the office." He picked up his clipboard and waved it in the air as though the jumble of purchase orders and diagrams would give her an explanation he could not. "My chief engineer quit on me. Last time I hire a foreigner. He was supposed to be bringing the freight elevator up to code so we could use it to transport heavier supplies and equipment to the upper floors. He said he couldn't do the work if I couldn't get him the right replacement parts. Does he know what kind of antique that thing is? You punt. You create parts that will work. You don't leave the job half-done."

"I used the freight elevator yesterday." To pay a disastrous visit to the hermit who lived in the penthouse. Maybe she'd taken an even bigger risk than she'd imagined. "Isn't it safe?"

"For passenger use, yeah. But I've got limestone blocks and marble trim ready to move. I'll either have to tear out a wall and lift it with a crane, or tell my men they have to transport it one brick at a time." He rubbed at his chest as though his heartburn was acting up again. "My crew will be quittin' in droves when I tell them that."

He seemed to be waiting for her to say something. "I guess good help is hard to find."

"Sane help is. I think he really quit because of the other thing."

"What other thing?"

"Said he heard voices in the elevator shaft. I think he gave in to the whole curse, jinx, bad-luck stories that are flying around this project. You tell me—have you ever heard voices in this building?"

"No."

"Superstitious nut job." J.T. was shaking his head. He picked up another forkful of beef and potatoes and stuffed it in his mouth. "I'm sorry about your friend. But I haven't seen him myself, and I don't have the manpower to spare to start searching for him. Now, please. I know you don't get much of a dinner crowd. You don't want to drive your only customer away, do you?"

Kit glanced around at the empty tables and counter waiting to be cleared. With twilight veiling the street outside, what passed for a dinner rush had already ended. She sighed with a different sort of worry. Twilight and the unbussed tables weren't just bad for business. It meant Matt hadn't shown up for work. Again.

"Miss Snow?" J.T. demanded a response.

Summoning a cordial smile, Kit buried her worry right next to where she'd tucked away her bruised ego after that unexpected, perspective-changing, completely misguided kiss she'd shared with Damon. "Milk, right. Could I get you some pie or ice cream to finish off that brisket?"

"If you've got a slice of coconut cream, I'll take it."

"Sure thing." Kit picked up an armload of plates and glasses from the next table and carried them back to the kitchen. After depositing them, she washed her hands and prepped the milk and dessert. "Hey, Germane?"

The tall black man straightened behind the grill where he'd been cleaning. "You got an order for me?"

"No. We're down to the last customer for the day, I think. Have you seen Matt yet?"

"I haven't heard a peep out of that boy." Germane went back to scraping the grill and had to raise his voice to be heard over the clash of metal on metal. "He sure was worried about you yesterday. I kind of figured he'd be stickin' closer to home for a while. He took it hard when your folks died. I think he thought he was gonna lose you, too."

"I'm tougher than he thinks."

"Maybe he's tougher than *you* think." The scraping stopped. "You know he offered to pay the hospital bill? In installments, of course."

She didn't know. "We have insurance for that. And I can come up with the money to meet the deductible."

Germane held up the scraper in surrender. "He just wanted to help. A man likes to take care of his family."

"A woman does, too." Kit squirted a swirl of whipped cream on top of the pie, which she was sure J.T. didn't need. The heavyset man was a heart attack waiting to happen. Maybe she should have suggested a lower-cholesterol alternative. But then, didn't she already have enough men in her life to worry about? "Damon said he thought Matt sounded like a responsible adult. I wonder what side my brother is showing to the rest of the world that he isn't showing me."

"Damon? Who's Damon?"

"Dr. Sinclair. He—" Kit stopped abruptly, with the pie plate poised above the serving tray. She set it down before she continued. "He came to see me in the hospital. He's the man Helen Hodges works for." She pointed to the ceiling, knowing her explanation was woefully inadequate for the twisted relationship she and Damon were working so hard *not* to share. "He lives in the penthouse upstairs."

"Rich old fart, is he?"

"His father might have been." Images of strong, dexterous hands and a tall, lean body sheathed in black blipped through her brain. Had Germane fired up the grill again? "This Dr. Sinclair is in his thirties. He may be a bit eccentric…" Okay, a lot eccentric. "But he's young and vital. Silver-haired. A brilliant inventor…" Germane was grinning from ear to ear. "What?"

"You know, your brother isn't the only one who disappears from this place for stretches at a time. Just where exactly was this *silver-haired* doctor when you took off with a basket of leftovers yesterday afternoon?"

Kit picked up the tray. "I wanted to thank him for helping me at the hospital. So I took him a free lunch. I thought he might be as concerned about building safety as I am."

"Handsome devil, is he?"

"You're half-right."

"Uh-huh. You were pretty flushed when you came back downstairs. And my barbecue sauce isn't that hot."

"We argued, okay?" She skipped the entire sweep-her-off-her-feet-and-kiss-her-senseless part of the visit and got to the issue that really counted. "Apparently, I've made a pest of myself, intruding on his life, messing with his routine. His work is everything to him, and he doesn't like to be disturbed."

Germane's teasing smile dimmed. "Was this guy rude to you? I don't care if he does own the building—I will talk with him. After all you do for folks around here—"

"It's okay. Really." Bless his heart for wanting to go to bat for her. But Germane's arthritic knees would put him at a distinct disadvantage against a man who created death serums and miracle cures, as well as the enemies who had no qualms about getting rid of anyone who stood in the way of obtaining those formulas for themselves. "I think the doctor and I have agreed to keep our distance from each other."

"You sure there's nothin' goin' on I need to worry about?"

"Besides little old ladies getting assaulted in our alley and homeless friends vanishing?" Kit reached across the counter to give Germane's arm a reassuring squeeze. "Trust me, old friend, Damon Sinclair is not our problem."

"If you say so." With both his curiosity and concern appeased for the moment, Germane patted her hand and went back to work. "Why don't you give that brother of yours a call in the meantime. That's what that cell phone's for, isn't it?"

Several minutes later, after Kronemeyer had gone and she'd cleared the tables, Kit pulled her cell phone from her apron pocket and slid into one of the booths at the front window. She punched in Matt's number and tucked the phone between her shoulder and ear while she lined up napkins and silverware to roll them up for the next day.

Other than Germane's tuneless singing in the kitchen, the phone ringing in her ear was the only sound she heard. The diner was dead now. With nightfall, the streetlights came on and Hannity's Bar across the street picked up some business. But she wouldn't see any more customers tonight unless one of Hannity's patrons needed some food to sober up or prevent a hangover.

Or if Henry should finally show up.

"C'mon, Matt. Answer."

If Matt had his phone turned on, he could alleviate her worry in a matter of seconds. If he didn't, then she'd be left with her imagination to create all sorts of terrible scenarios. He'd missed his bus. He'd been hurt. He was roaming the streets with a gang and getting himself into trouble. He was making time in the backseat of some girl's car. Or he wasn't doing anything risky at all—he just resented Kit and her rules so much that—

"Yo."

Yo?

She'd never heard her brother talk like that before. Was that music playing? And that mechanical hum in the background was familiar.

But out of context over the phone, she couldn't place it. "Who is this?"

"Who is *this?*" This voice was full of swagger and flirt, definitely not her brother's style.

"Sorry, I must have the wrong number."

"You call me anytime, baby."

Unimpressed with the lothario's charm, Kit hung up and checked the number on her phone. That had to be right. This time she dialed the number manually. It picked up after one ring.

"Yo. Miss me already, baby?"

She wasn't amused. "Where is Matt Snow?"

"Who?" The noisy background still made no sense.

"I believe you're using his phone."

"And I believe you might be my destiny."

Kit snapped the phone shut and disconnected the call. "What is going on?" Had Matt loaned his phone to a friend? Had it been stolen?

The next thing she knew, *her* phone was ringing. Kit answered. "Hello?"

"You know, babe, I believe in fate. You could come meet me down—"

"You're not my type." She automatically hung up on the crank call, then turned off her phone. "Thank God."

But it wasn't good riddance that earned her thanks. It was welcome home. Kit knocked on the window, trying to get the attention of the man outside. He shuffled along the sidewalk across the street, shoulders hunched down against the cold. He wore a red-and-gold Kansas City Chiefs parka and carried a black backpack slung across his shoulder.

A wave of relief washed over her, easing the tension in her gut. Matt was home, safe and sound.

Kit scooted out of the booth. She needed a hug first. Then she'd get some answers. And make him wash the dishes. No, they'd wash them together. That way, any reminders she made about checking in and being responsible would come across as conversation and not a lecture. Heck, she just wanted to spend the time with him.

"Matt?"

He paused at the steps in front of Hannity's. He looked over his shoulder, looked ahead into the night beyond the streetlamp. Looked across the street at the Sinclair Building, at the neon sign marking Snow's Barbecue. At her.

Kit waved. Sort of. She stuck her hand into the air, but curled her fingers into her palm and pulled it back when he didn't respond. Why was he just standing there?

His face was shadowed by his fur-trimmed hood, his features obscured by white clouds of warm breath in the cold air. But she knew that coat. Knew that backpack.

Was something wrong? What was he waiting for?

Why was *she* waiting? Kit hurried to the door. "Matt?"

The figure turned away and climbed the concrete steps, disappearing into Hannity's Bar. Of all the stupid, irritating… He had to have seen her. She shoved open the door and ran out onto the sidewalk. "Matt!"

A blast of cold wind absorbed her shout. But it didn't make any difference. He was gone. She'd give him the benefit of the doubt for not hearing her—he was probably blasting music in his earphones. But she couldn't excuse the choice he'd made. What's an eighteen-year-old doing in a bar?

Kit hurried back into the diner, grabbed her quilted jacket off the coatrack, and shrugged into it as she called back to the kitchen. "I'm running an errand across the street, Germane. Go ahead and lock up when you're done."

"I'll keep an eye on things. Don't you worry."

But Kit was already out the door. She darted between two parked cars and crossed the empty street. She was up the steps and inside Hannity's before she ever got her coat zipped.

Just inside the door, the darkness stopped her. The stale smells of spilled beer, old smoke and the cleanser that couldn't quite cover it all stung her nose. While her eyes adjusted to the "atmosphere," her ears picked up a couple of conversations that were loud enough to be heard over the jukebox. Two men raising the stakes over a game of pool. Another man trying to coax a blonde who was too smart to listen onto his lap.

Why on earth would Matt come into this place? Was this sinkhole where he'd been spending all his unaccounted-for time? She hadn't smelled it on his clothes, but still…

"Over here, honey." An Irish drawl called to her from behind the bar. "You look lost."

Kit crossed to the bar but didn't pull up a seat. She was scanning the pool tables and patrons on the stools beside her. Though she recognized members of Kronemeyer's construction crew, there was no sign of Matt. "I'm looking for my brother."

The jockey-size bartender slapped a coaster in front of her. "You're that bird from across the street. Are they ever gonna get that work finished on the Sinclair? Didn't know you had a brother. What'll you have?"

"Nothing, thanks. He's six feet tall, has spiky brown hair. He's wearing a Chiefs parka."

"We get a lot of football fans in here on the weekends. Beer?"

Kit shook her head, trying to peer into each dark wooden booth across the room. "He just came in a minute ago. He'd be underage."

"Not in my bar, he wouldn't." Hannity's was known for plain drinks, plain talk, and no questions asked. She'd just broken all three rules. "You're welcome to look around all you want. But if you sit at the bar, you have to buy a drink."

"Thanks, anyway. Do you have any back rooms or—"

There. A glimpse of red slipping around the corner from the hallway next to the restrooms. "Matt!"

He disappeared without responding to her call.

At least he wasn't carrying a drink.

Kit dashed through the archway after him. The flat-screen TVs in here were all tuned to different sporting events. Had he come into Hannity's to watch some college basketball?

Curiosity had already become concern and was quickly moving its way toward angry frustration. There were dozens of Chiefs emblems in the room—arrowheads on the walls, helmets on the shelves. Red shirts. White shirts. When she finally spotted the only moving logo, it was headed out the emergency exit door.

"Matthew Allan Snow!"

If her shout didn't earn her a glare from every man in the room, then the blaring buzz of the open-door alarm would. "Sorry."

Hot on his trail now, Kit didn't stop to apologize again. She burst through the exit into the alley behind the bar. It was cold. Dark. Empty. Other than trash cans and power poles, there was nothing here. Her brother was gone. She didn't need to be here any more than he did.

"Start walkin', girl," she chided herself, flashing back to memories of Helen's attack and feeling a shiver that had nothing to do with the icy temps.

There'd been a man in a Chiefs parka then, too, stooping over Helen—more interested in the contents of her purse than the woman bleeding at his feet. There'd been a smaller man beside him, snapping orders. Small as in jockey-size?

Kit slowly turned and backed away from the steel door, as though the enemy was watching her from the other side. She'd spotted the two men outside Hannity's shortly before the attack. And a third one had appeared out of nowhere to slam her against the wall.

Maybe she wasn't as alone as she thought.

Lengthening her stride, Kit hurried to the relative safety of the sidewalk out front. Even if the exit hadn't already locked behind her, she had no intention of going back in that place. But there was no red parka to be found out here, either.

"Dammit, Matt. What's going on?"

Maybe she hadn't been chasing her brother at all. But why stop to make eye contact with her? Like the man she pursued had done, Kit looked up and down the block. There were only a handful of people out and about on the bitter night—a couple of Henry's friends, digging through the trash at the corner, a car leaving the parking garage and nearly colliding with a city bus as it swung around the Kronemeyer dump truck parked on the street, another man heading up Hannity's front steps.

Kit pulled on her gloves and tied her scarf around her neck, trying to see the scene through the eyes of the man in the parka. The diner was the brightest spot on the block. With all its windows, he had to have spotted her. If it had been Matt in that coat, why not just come home?

If it hadn't, then what was he looking for?

The Sinclair Tower, wrapped up in its wintry coat of scaffolding and plastic and mystery, offered no answers. She saw no signs of movement at any window, and only the lights from the diner and Kronemeyer's first-floor office gave any indication that people lived and worked there.

Kit tipped her face up into the starless night, up toward Damon's sky-high prison. There was a solitary light shining way up there as well. What was Damon doing now? Fixing a late dinner? Writing out equations? Thriving on his loneliness? Forgetting about her?

She couldn't understand it. How could a man

with so much to offer the world lock himself away from it? Was he really so hung up on his harsh looks? So hurt by the honest responses of human interaction? Or was that sensitivity just an easy excuse to avoid conversations and compassion and caring?

How could a man who held her hand so surely, and watched over her like a guard dog while she lay in a hospital bed, turn around and treat the most completely seductive kiss of her life like a failed science experiment?

If she closed her eyes and imagined, she was being swept away by a fierce pirate. But if she opened her eyes—as his practical nature demanded she should—she was in the arms of a very real, very complicated man. Damaged by life inside and out. But so utterly masculine—so gruff, strong, sexy…

A squeal of brakes and hiss of air dragged her attention back down to the reality of the street where she had to live. *The bus.*

Not so out of context now.

Trusting an instinct, Kit walked toward the end of the block. That was the sound she'd heard on the phone. The mechanical drone of the engine, the conversations and music of passengers on-board.

The bus had stopped at the corner, trading off weary working people for nighttime revelers heading south toward the nightlife of the Plaza. She pulled her phone from her apron, turned it on and speed-dialed Matt's number.

"Don't answer," she whispered, walking faster and praying she was wrong. "Don't pick up."

"Yo. Change your mind about me, baby? H'lo?"

Kit ran to catch the bus. He was there. Climbing the steps and taking a seat.

Breathless from the cold as much as the chase, she reached the front door just as it was closing. She knocked on the glass and the driver let her in. "Thanks."

She dug the necessary change from her apron and wove her way to the back of the bus to find a seat. *Chiefs parka, second row from the rear.* Kit listened to her phone and watched the young, twentysomething Asian man say the exact words she heard in her ear. "Don't toy with me, baby." They hung up together.

Kit sat down across the aisle from him, saw the black backpack at his feet, embroidered with the initials MS, a rare surviving example of her mother's needlework. The coat probably had her own less-skilled stitching on its label.

He pulled back the hood, scratched his fingers through the scruffy mess of raven-colored hair on his head and smiled at her.

"I'm Kenny."

"Kit Snow. You have my brother's things."

That's when she saw the tip of the gun, pointing at her from the end of one bulky, oversize sleeve. "And I have you."

Guess she was taking a trip to the Plaza.

"HELLO, MR. BLACK HOLE." Damon turned the com-puter screen to watch his unseen nemesis launch his opening maneuvers to gain access into the SinPharm database. Now the game would begin—bypassing security walls, decrypting codes, searching through level after level on the SinPharm site for the most restricted areas that held Damon's research in their translated form. "You're early tonight."

Early or not, he was ready. After watching the admirable savvy of his opponent quickly getting through the first two levels of encryption, Damon launched his own counter program. While Black Hole of the Universe hacked his way deeper and deeper into Damon's system, Damon was quietly worming his way into his.

During the last online attack, Damon had been able to determine that the hacker was right here in Kansas City. Tonight he intended to find out exactly what building, what room, what keyboard the spy was using. Then Damon intended to pay his online pal a live and in-his-face visit.

Finding the hacker would put him that much

closer to finding who was so hell-bent on stealing his work and destroying his life. Damon wasn't sure how yet, but he was dead certain that payback would be painful and thorough and swift.

"That should keep you busy for a while."

With his computer program activated, Damon rolled his stool back over to the work station to analyze the agar in petri dish #K26 beneath the microscope again. Kit—26 years old. His newest donor to his Miranda's Formula research.

He held his breath as he placed his eye against the scope. That couldn't be right. Damon leaned back, rubbed any trace of fatigue from his eye and looked again. "Son of a bitch."

The blood rushed to his head and pounded in his ears just as fiercely as it had when he'd let go of his sanity and kissed Kit.

He pulled another light over to study the sample again. "One. Two. Three. Four."

He took a deep breath and scraped his palm across the late night stubble on his chin. It was real. It was real! Kit had insisted that reality was more important than any dream. She was some damn fine kind of reality plowing into his life.

She should see this.

Kit was the reality that had made this happen.

Damon crossed to the scribbled equations that covered the white boards along an entire wall in his lab. He picked up a marker and circled the answer. Added an exclamation point. Wrote out K26 and stepped back, feeling the adrenaline rush transform itself into a quieter, more reverent energy inside him.

K26.

Kit Snow.

"You're the miracle, sweetheart."

In more ways than he could ever fully document.

Being the practical scientist he was, Damon tabled his emotional reaction to his discovery and quickly sat down at an independent computer terminal to record the equations, results and observations on the K26 experiment. He'd encrypt them and print them out later.

Right now he needed to share the news with Kit. Would she appreciate what this could mean? Her background in chemistry would help her understand the terminology. But would she want to hear anything from him? Could she accept that he wanted to share this—his work—with her? But that he couldn't share, that she wouldn't want… that his work was all he *could* give her?

Damon rolled his stool over to the camera monitors to search for her. She wasn't in the diner. In fact, Germane was locking the doors and turning out the lights. Damon had no way of knowing if she was even home. Not wanting to acknowledge his disappointment at not being able to see her, Damon shifted the cameras to their normal security views and made a mental note to have Easting call Kit in the morning to arrange a meeting with her. Damon could put his findings in a report and Easting could deliver…

"What the hell?" The camera that watched the building's main entrance had picked up a familiar figure wandering out of the alley across the street.

Kit's breath in the cold air obscured her face, but he recognized the ponytail and the curve of the jeans. She was on her phone, looking down the sidewalk. Damon swung the camera around to follow the direction of her gaze.

A man in a Chiefs parka.

Matching her description of the man who'd assaulted Helen.

Getting on a bus at the corner.

And Kit was running after him!

Damon shot to his feet. "Does that woman have a death wish?"

And where was the security guard Easting had assigned to her?

"Stop! Dammit, woman." Kit was actually getting onto the bus with the man she'd followed down the sidewalk.

Damon memorized the route number of the bus

on the monitor and shed his lab coat. If his latest variation of Miranda's Formula wasn't showing that slight but significant promise, he'd be out the door already.

But he had to protect the work.

He had to protect the miracle.

He was half-afraid to move the petri dish. Almost afraid to leave it at all, in case the four new skin cells growing there turned out to be another cruel dementia from his nightmares.

"Reality, Doc." Kit Snow wanted a neighbor who'd step out the door if she ever got into trouble. And he had a very bad feeling that she was in it up to her eyeballs.

He looked one more time before locking the K26 sample inside the sterile vault. The cells hadn't mutated. They hadn't died. The rejection factors he'd studied in Kit's bloodwork may have provided the key he'd been looking for.

His formula just might work.

But what kind of redemption would that be if finding Miranda's cure cost him the life of another woman?

One who seemed to have some damn illogical ideas about how to take care of herself. One who seemed to think that she could change the world if she just stepped in front of the speeding freight train often enough.

Damon locked down the lab and boarded the elevator. As soon as he pressed the ground floor button, the car lurched on its cable. "Son of a—"

Bracing his hands against the walls, he held on as the elevator shuddered around him. It dropped six inches. Caught. And then, with the metallic whine of steel straining against steel, the gears ground together and the elevator began its normal descent.

If this thing had ever shown any signs of life, he'd be dissecting it in his lab right now.

Damon pulled his cell phone from his coat. J. T. Kronemeyer would be his second call. Sin-Pharm headquarters was his first.

"Easting." No sense wasting time with pleasantries. "Which of your security team is supposed to be watching Katherine Snow right now?"

"I'm in the middle of a meeting, Damon. Remember? Japanese delegation? Kenichi Corp investors?" Irritation colored Easting's voice. "I don't have that information in front of me right now."

"Get the name," Damon ordered. "And tell him to clear out his desk."

"Is there a problem?"

"If anything happens to Kit there will be."

Easting's tone changed. "I'll get right on it." He picked up another line and put a call through to his assistant. "What else do you need?"

"Find the route for city bus 2705. I want to know every stop it makes south of Eighteenth Street."

"You're not…riding the bus, are you?" Was that surprise that he was leaving the penthouse before midnight? Or that he was planning to do some serious interacting with the outside world? "I can send a car for you."

"I have a car." Damon hadn't quite considered what he was about to do, either. But like any challenging equation, he'd figure it out before he was done. "Transfer the information to this number as soon as you have it."

"Do you want me to dispatch another guard?"

"No." The elevator door opened. "I'll handle it."

Damon closed his phone and passed through the lobby into the night.

Mental note: Lock Kit Snow in her room. Better yet, lock her in mine.

It was the only way he could keep her from investigating things on her own and putting herself in the line of fire.

It was the only way he could stop the fear that twisted in his stomach. Fear that his world had forever tarnished hers.

Fear that he couldn't keep her safe from his enemies.

Or her own good intentions.

Chapter Nine

Kenny-with-the-almond-eyes linked his arm through Kit's, jammed the barrel of his gun into the folds of her coat and guided her off the bus at Forty-seventh Street.

During the holiday season between Thanksgiving and New Year's, the old-monied Country Club Plaza area of Kansas City was one of the most popular shopping and tourist destinations in the Midwest. But in the drudge of January weather, the boutiques, art museums and specialty restaurants belonged to the locals. The shops closed early, the parking lots were half empty, and the sidewalks that once teemed with musicians, artists and holiday shoppers were nearly deserted.

"What did you do to Matt?" Kit asked, stepping off the curb and sinking into a crystallized snowbank. The cold water that soaked into her boots didn't chill her so much as the gleeful smile that never left his face. He had a gun, an attitude, and he hadn't answered one of her questions.

"C'mon, babe." As Kenny tugged her on across the four-lane street, Kit sized up whether he was tall enough to have been the man who'd injected her with the 428 serum at the hospital. But poor Kenny was a shrimp, not any taller than she was. No wonder he exuded all that bravado. Could he have been the shorter man who'd attacked Helen? Maybe this abduction had nothing to do with either of the attacks on Helen or her.

Maybe Kit was just having a very bad week.

"I don't think a boy with zits on his chin should be calling me *babe*." Or carrying weapons or messing with her life. "Where's Matt?"

He answered by jabbing the gun into a rib and bruising her, then laughing at her hiss of pain as they passed another couple strolling past. "All you were supposed to do was follow me out of the diner."

"Why?"

"Because we wanted you out of the diner. Duh."

"Who's we?"

Kenny swore at how easily he'd slipped. Obviously he wasn't the brainy partner of whomever the "we" consisted of. "In here." He shoved her toward a bank of windows surrounding the stairs and escalators that led to the different floors of a multistory mall. "Go down."

By the time they'd descended two levels on the escalators, Kit could see the sweat beading on Kenny's upper lip. They hadn't been inside long enough to warm up yet. That young man was nervous. An observation that emboldened Kit to keep talking.

"Why did you need me out of the diner?" Germane would be closing up, then heading to his apartment on the second floor. Was he safe?

"We have…" He wiped the sweat on the parka sleeve, then ground the gun into the same sore spot again, just to remind her who the tough guy was here. "There's work to be done."

"You're part of the construction team working on remodeling the building?" Not likely. He was anything but a burly, calloused construction worker.

"Shut up. In here." He stopped at the entrance to the Black Hole Internet Café and ushered her inside.

A modern cousin to Hannity's Bar, the Black Hole was dark and crowded. The air smelled of coffee rather than booze, and the sounds were more hushed, but Kit still had a sense that there was something in the shadows waiting for her. Something she needed to find and understand before it was too late.

At each round table, there was a small lamp and a computer. At each seating group, there were plug-ins and access ports where personal laptops could be used. Kenny led her to a sofa back in the darkest corner, where only the strings of star lights on the walls and ceiling provided any illumination. A pair of college-age girls hovered nearby, debating whether they should set their mugs or their butts down first. Kenny made the decision for them. "Move."

Kit supposed that from the shadows, even a runt with a zit on his chin could intimidate if he dropped his voice to the right pitch.

The girls took off in a huff, and Kenny pushed Kit down on the cushions and took a seat beside her. "What is going on here?" she demanded. "Tell me about Matt. Is he okay? Did you hurt him?"

"I need to make a call first. Then we'll discuss Matty."

Matty? Kenny-wanna-be-a-big-man knew her brother well enough to call him by his nickname?

Oh, God, Matty. What have you gotten yourself into?

Kenny plopped Matt's backpack on the coffee table and pulled out a laptop, a second box that looked like some type of battery pack with an antenna, a handful of wires and Matt's cell phone. He dialed a number and tucked the phone against his ear while he plugged in the computer and connected all the accessories with a casual speed which indicated that what Kenny didn't know about keeping his mouth shut, he did know about computers.

"Yo. It's me." His call must have picked up. "You won't believe who I got sittin' beside me here at work."

Work? Kenny worked at the Black Hole? That explained the computer savvy.

His good humor faded. "You said our location had been compromised so I moved. I have the equipment here to set it up, and with my relay station in place, no one will be able to trace the source to us." He swore. "Fine. To *me*.

"You said you needed to get her out of that place, and the opportunity was there, so I took it." From the sound of things, someone was attacking Kenny Shrimp's manhood. "If I was more like my father, then I'd be a helluva lot poorer and you wouldn't have me on your team. Hey, my father turned down your offer as I recall. You needed a man with *my* vision to make this thing work." He groaned. "I'm on it, already. Just give me a minute."

He booted up the laptop and snapped his fingers to summon a waitress from the bar. While Kenny multitasked away, Kit took in every detail—from the short e-mail he read and responded to from a fellow Black Hole of the Universe address, to the lines of programming scrolling down the screen, to the way he pulled the pistol from Matt's parka sleeve and slipped it into the waistband of his jeans.

"How do you know my brother?" Kit ventured to ask during a lull while Kenny waited for the response to a command.

"He comes in here sometimes."

Matt hung out at a place like this? Not with a gang, as she'd feared, but with…computer geeks? Of course, this particular geek seemed to be doing something that wasn't entirely legal on his souped-up laptop. And to her knowledge, Matt had never carried a gun. "Is Matty okay?"

"The truth is out there," Kenny leaned over and whispered, patting the gun at his stomach. "Just remember it's gonna stay out there if you try anything I don't want you to."

He tapped the end of her nose with his fingertip and Kit had to clench her hands into fists in her lap to keep from slapping it away. "Where is Matt?"

The perky waitress from the bar came over and laid two napkins on the table. "Do you want the usual, Mr. Kenichi?"

Kenny held up one hand to silence her while he typed in commands with the other. "Karma's right tonight, baby. You're gonna be mine." He pressed Enter, grinned with satisfaction, then tipped a grin up to their waitress. "Yeah, Sally. Bring one for the lady, too."

"Two Galaxy Specials coming up."

Whatever that was, Kit wasn't having any. She

unzipped her jacket and scooted forward to remove it. But Kenny was instantly there, pushing her back into the cushions and leaning over her. Kit caught her breath and held it. He had a hand on her shoulder and the gun pressed beneath her breast. "I said don't try anything."

Was it so dark in this place that no one could see the danger she was in? Was he such a well-loved or well-feared boss that no one dared to get in his way? He drew the gun along the curve of her breast in a sick simulation of a caress. "Unless this is what you wanted?" His dark-brown eyes glittered with a game she didn't want to play. "I have to finish work first, baby. But I can oblige you later."

Though her stomach roiled at his suggestive touch, she wisely fought back the urge to shove him off her. "I was just getting comfortable. Is that okay?"

"Okay." She didn't breathe until the gun disappeared and Kenny backed away. As he slowly retreated, she sat up and curled her right leg beneath her. She wedged her coat beneath her, too, propping herself up higher. He watched every movement, nodding his approval when she finally settled.

In reality Kit wanted to be high enough so that she could get a look at the other customers over the backs of sofas and chairs. *He comes in here sometimes.* One of them might be Matt.

The laptop beeped, and Kenny twisted away as though he'd been paged. Sparing Kit one more look to keep her in her seat, he pulled the phone back to his mouth and leaned over his keyboard. "We're in. Oh, yeah, tonight's gonna be the night."

With the high-backed seats surrounding pools of light, it was hard to make out more than the silhouettes of people's heads. Curly hair. Straight hair. Ball cap. Stocking cap. But no scruffy spikes of hair that reminded her of Matt.

It wasn't so much a matter of Kenny leading her to Matt, anymore. Now she wanted to find Matt first, and get him away from Kenny.

If it wasn't already too late.

She squelched that possibility back to the pit of her stomach and kept searching.

Short hair. No hair. Long hair. Wait. Kit's gaze returned to the wingback chair in the group closest to them. But no, it had to be a trick of the light. Someone was wearing glasses with a strap holding them on. That silly little surge of hope was pointless. There was no dark guardian of the shadows to bail her out of this one. She'd gotten herself into this mess. Now she'd have to get herself—and Matt—out of it on her own.

"Two Galaxy Specials."

Kit cradled the coffee concoction the waitress brought them between her hands. Kenny was typing furiously now, and Kit wondered if she could do more damage dumping the steaming brew over his head or into his lap.

She did neither, once she saw what Kenny was working on. A round, green-and-white logo flashed at the top left corner of his screen. The giant *S* was instantly recognizable. SinPharm. Sinclair Pharmaceuticals. Restricted: Password Required.

Kenny Yo-Baby was hacking into the SinPharm database. "What…?"

He turned expectantly, and she quickly averted her eyes to the steam rising from her mug. "What's in this? It's not bad."

"Coffee and enough syrup and sugar to get your juices runnin'—if you know what I mean." The party at the other end of the phone interrupted Kenny's attempt to flirt. He swore in a language as foreign to Kit as the Far East, and as familiar as the alley behind her restaurant. He was one of Helen's attackers! But before Kit could decide what to do with that information, he'd returned his full attention to the call. "No, I am not talking to you. Give me a break. Yes, I'm down to level two now. What you want is next." He typed in a new command and his screen went blank. "Wait for it. Yes!"

Green numbers and letters spun at the center of the screen, rolling to a stop and aligning themselves one at a time like a Vegas slot machine. From the dancing Kenny was doing in his seat, he'd hit the jackpot.

"Told you I was the best. And Dad wanted to send me back to school." Was Kenny talking to one of the other attackers? He slid a glance at Kit. "She's still here. Well it worked, didn't it? Fine. I'll call you when I'm there." He hung up and stuffed the phone into his pocket. "Make me a million dollars, baby. Oh, yeah, I'm two steps ahead of him tonight."

The letters and numbers created a pattern that began to make more sense with every symbol that was added on.

A code. He was decrypting and downloading some kind of code. What did beating up little old ladies and computer hacking have to do with each other?

"C'mon, Matty. Make it stick."

Kit's thoughts shifted on a single word. "Matty?"

"Didn't I tell you? Your brother and I have been working on a project together." Kenny thumbed the zipper of the Chiefs parka he wore. "He's even paying me for the privilege."

"No." The clipped denial was out before Kit could consider the wisdom of starting an argument with a man carrying a gun. "Matt wouldn't break the law." She pointed toward the laptop. "What you're doing is illegal."

"So turn me in." Kenny laughed. "Baby bro will be sittin' in the cell right next to me."

"Where is he? What have you done to him?"

Only three more numbers were waiting to spin into place. Kenny watched the screen as he leaned back and snuggled against her. Kit tightened her fingers around her mug. Coffee in the lap was looking better and better all the time. He trailed a finger up her arm. "Matty came to me on a gift platter one day. Just like you did tonight."

"He doesn't know what you're doing is illegal."

"He might not. But he's so psyched to get to play on all my equipment that he probably wouldn't care."

Two numbers were left spinning on the screen.

"What do you mean he's paying for the privilege? What equipment are you talking about?"

The finger drifted over her collarbone and headed for a breast. "Matt's a natural talent. Didn't he tell you? He's been coming to the Black Hole for about a year now. He's a self-taught computer genius. Of course, unless you bring your own tools, you have to pay to play. He had some money from an inheritance he was using, but that ran out after a while. I offered him a job, but he said his sister and schoolwork were demanding too much of his time. Shame on you."

He palmed her breast through her sweater and Kit flinched, sloshing coffee over the sides of her mug. She let the liquid scald her fingers as her loathing burned deep.

"Easy now." Kenny took the mug and set it on the table. He curled his fingers around her arm and played with her wrist. *Do not touch my hand. Do not try to hold my hand!* The symbolic violation would be worse than any other adolescent grope he'd tried thus far. "It's not your fault. He said he had a full-ride scholarship to go to some fancy school like my father wanted to send me to. That it was your parents' dream, your dream. Just like it was my father's dream. But it's not ours."

"Matty is nothing like you. He's a confused teenager."

The last number on the screen continued to spin.

"I think he knows exactly what he wants. When his money runs out at the end of the month, you know how he pays me? In trade." A coat. A phone. A backpack. Helping Kenny hack into SinPharm's computer system.

Kit was going to be ill.

"Whatever he owes you, I'll pay it. Don't ask him to do this."

"You can't offer the kind of money I'm making off this deal." He reached the back of her hand. "Unless you want to work out some sort of trade, too."

The numbers and letters exploded across the screen and drifted off the bottom of the picture. Kit snatched her hand away and covered her mouth to stifle a yelp of almost hysteric laughter. "Your program just crashed."

"What?" Kenny shoved her aside and attacked his computer, typing frantically. But the numbers kept drifting away. "No. No!"

While he was so furiously distracted, Kit was quietly sliding away. Then a familiar crop of hair popped up from a chair near the coffee bar and she froze. "Matt?"

He pulled earphones from his ears as he gathered up a spiral notebook and pen and hurried toward them. "I'm sorry, man. I lost the stream. I think if we…Kit." The intense concentration that lined his forehead lifted in surprise. "What are you doing here?"

He was alive and unhurt. Thank God. "What are *you* doing?"

"Son of a bitch." Kenny's screen was blank. "I had it. I had it!"

Clearly confused by Kit's appearance, Matt stumbled over his words. "Who's watchin' the diner? I didn't call, I know. This took longer than

I, um…here." He turned to Kenny and pointed to a line in his notes. "In this cell, there was a booby trap in the last level, and—"

"I don't want your frickin' notes!" Kenny leaped to his feet and knocked the papers from Matt's hand. "Get back on your computer and we'll do it again."

"But if we don't adjust…"

Kenny was reaching inside the parka. His gun!

Kit jumped up, damning the foot that had gone to sleep beneath her. "I need you at home. Now." She clipped her shin on the coffee table and nearly cried at her inability to get Matt out of there fast enough. She tried to push him away as she stumbled. "Go. Just go."

"Nobody's leaving." Kenny grabbed Kit's arm and jerked her back to his side. He wasn't making any effort to hide the gun he jabbed into her ribs.

Matt's eyes widened. "Hey. Is that a—?"

The waitress saw the gun and screamed.

"Go, Matt," Kit begged. "Please."

Patrons were rising from their seats—searching for the danger, trading questions, sharing warnings—blindly backing away from the unknown threat.

Kenny jabbed harder. "Get on your computer and run the damn program."

"I'm not an idiot, you know. I knew this was illegal. I just wanted to see if I could do it. And I can." Matt, bless his stupid heart, chose now to stand his ground and go all protective brother on her. "Put the gun down and let her go. Or I won't tell you where you made your mistake in the program."

"Me? You wouldn't know jack if I hadn't helped you out." He swung his arm out and aimed the gun at Matt. "Now run it again and get me the frickin' codes!"

"He has a gun!"

"Matt!" Shouted warnings and calls for 911 turned the nervous shadows into a blind panic. A lamp broke. Some started running for the door.

"Kit?"

Dammit, he was only eighteen! "Don't be a hero."

"I hate the diner. It reminds me of—"

"I know."

"I wasn't really gonna steal anything."

"It's okay." *Go.*

"I don't want to lose—"

Kenny dragged her in front of him and ground the gun into her temple. "Will you two shut the—"

A tall, dark figure separated itself from the chaos.

Kenny's arm jerked and twisted. He yelped in pain. Broad shoulders knocked Kit aside, blocking everything from sight but a fortress of black leather. "Damon?"

Whatever scuffle took place was waist-high and brief. She heard curses and grunts. And a gunshot. Damon jerked.

"Damon!"

Her shout could barely be heard over the screams of the crowd. She reached out to him, but Matt pulled her away from the fight.

The two men froze. Damon stood a head taller, leaving poor Kenny gaping at his collar.

"I shot you," Kenny whined above the chaos of the crowd. "You were right there. I couldn't miss."

Damon slammed Kenny into the wall. He braced his forearm against his windpipe, lifted him off his feet and let him hang there. "Unless you want *me* to pull the trigger next time, you stay away from this family."

Now *that* was how a voice did intimidation.

Kenny's hands inched out on both sides in unspoken surrender.

Still anchoring Kenny to the wall with his right arm, Damon lowered the gun down to his left side. Kit frowned at the odd sight. He was holding it backward, with his fingers curved around the barrel, not the grip. A dark, shiny liquid coated his knuckles.

Blood.

"Damon." Kit charged forward.

She touched his arm but he shrugged her off. "It doesn't hurt."

"You've been shot. You need to see a doc—"

"I *am* a doctor. I'm fine." Damon glanced over his shoulder to Matt as he tucked the gun into the back of his black jeans. "Get your coat. Get your sister. And get out of here."

Matt pulled his parka off Kenny, who glared with resentment at being outnumbered and out-maneuvered.

"C'mon." Matt nudged Kit toward the logger-head of men and women trying to squeeze through the front door. "If he says go, I'm going."

Kit dodged around her brother and pulled out her cell to dial 911. "You go. This is a crime scene. I'm not leaving until we talk to the police and Damon's checked out by paramedics."

"Talk to the police outside," the growly voice ordered. "I need to have a little chat with this scumbag."

Damon's blood dripped onto the carpet. As the other patrons flocked to the exit, Kit was drawn to this dark corner, caught up in the confluence of dangerous energy that, like the café's namesake, surrounded him. She wanted to touch him, thank him, help him. "I'm not leaving without you."

He didn't seem to grasp *no*. "There are keys in my left coat pocket. My car's parked out front. A Lexus."

"I'll send Matt out there to wait."

"Katherine—"

"I'm not leaving." She slipped her hand inside his warm pocket for the keys, trying not to think how personal it was to have permission to reach inside anything that belonged to Damon. "The black one?"

"Yes. How—"

"Please." The man in black from eye to toe? She dropped the keys into Matt's hand. "Go on. You'll be safer outside. Lock yourself in."

"We just met this guy a few days ago. Are you sure we can trust him? I mean, geez, Kit, how does he know where to find you all the time?"

Kit let a little blip of suspicion slide, and pushed Matt toward the crowd at the door. "We're the ones he has no reason to trust. He has the right to be angry that…" She caught herself before saying *you*. She'd leave that discussion for later. "…that someone was hacking into the Sinclair Pharmaceuticals database."

"He didn't get in." Damon thrust his forearm up beneath Kenny's chin. "Mr. Black Hole in the Universe is good. But I'm better."

Dangling against the wall, Kenny clutched at Damon's arm. "How did you track me down?"

"Simple addition. Your online name plus the 2705 bus stop a couple blocks away. Who are you working for?"

"How do you know I'm not runnin' solo?"

"Because you're not bright enough." Damon

was shaking his head. "You look familiar. But I don't know you." He spoke over his shoulder without glancing her way. "If you're going to stay, get his wallet."

Kenny shook his head. "There are scarier people than you out there in the world."

"Don't count on it. Did you hurt Helen Hodges?"

"I got nothin' to say."

Kit did. She read the information from his billfold. "Ken Kenichi, Jr. From Japan. He has a student visa."

"Ken's son? Is he involved in this? We've done business for years."

"My father's an idiot for not seeing the opportunity here. He'd rather follow you than take the lead himself."

"You didn't do this on your own. Who do you work for?" Kenny rolled his eyes and looked away. Damon tightened his hold. "Who do you work for?"

Kit scooped up the laptop and shook it at Kenny. "We'll show this to the police if you don't answer our questions. You'll be the only one going to prison."

"Bite me."

Matt piped up from behind her. "Actually, you could probably get some names, or at least trace back to the locations of his contacts off that laptop."

"Screw you." Kenny spat the words at Matt.

Kit turned on Matt. "These are dangerous people we're dealing with. Why are you still here?"

"Quit treatin' me like a kid, Kit. Look, I take responsibility for my actions. I was helping Kenny hack into SinPharm. Okay?" He reached for the laptop. "I can probably pull some addresses off—"

"What's that?" A pinpoint beam of red light struck the computer an instant before the bullet did. "Matt!"

The plastic housing exploded in Matt's hand. A shard nicked Kit's cheek.

Her brother jumped back.

Kit whirled around.

She saw nothing. Heard nothing but screams of panic.

The red laser light swung back and forth, seeking another target.

Kit grabbed Matt's arm, but Damon was already diving for the floor, pulling them both down with him.

Silent bullets from the shadows rocketed over their heads and popped into the wall.

Lights and plaster shattered, raining debris over them. Kit buried her face in Matt's back. Damon's weight on top sandwiched them both to the floor. Kit latched on to the sleeve of his coat and pulled his hand in close to her chest. She wound her fingers through his and held on tight while the world crashed down around them.

Endless moments later the barrage had stopped. Most of the crowd had filtered through the exit, too focused on their own need for safety to even be aware of the attack. Sirens approached in the distance. Dust and smoke hung in the air.

"You two in one piece?" Damon's voice was a rusty reassurance against her ear.

Kit nodded. "Matt?"

"Yeah. Fine."

Kit's breath rushed out in one painful gasp, as though she'd been holding it through every second of the shooting. "Did you see who had the gun?"

Damon's warmth and protection shifted off her. "No. Too many people, too dark, too distracted."

"Why were they shooting at us?"

"Maybe because you ask too many questions?" His bloodied fingers never left hers as he helped her to their feet. "Now can I get you out of here?"

"Let me see your wound." She turned his hand between her palms.

"Kenny grazed me with his shot. It'll mend." He pulled a white handkerchief from his pocket to stanch the wound.

"I'll do it." Kit tied the cloth around his knuckles. "You'll need stitches to close that."

"No, I won't." He lifted a finger to the gash in her cheek. "You'll need one for that, though."

She thought she imagined a caress in his clinical touch. "Why me and not you?"

"Um, guys?" They both turned to Matt's voice. He'd picked up the two largest pieces of the shattered laptop. "We're not gettin' anything off this computer. It's toast."

Kit shivered. "So is he."

Damon's arm slid around her shoulders as the three of them stood and stared at the bright red dot of blood in the middle of Kenny Kenichi's forehead. It trickled down his nose as his dead body sank to the floor.

There were plenty of questions to be asked.

But someone had made sure there would be no answers tonight.

"SHOULD I BE WORRIED?"

It was a legitimate question. Cleaning the gun that had just committed another murder would make any man nervous. "Young Mr. Kenichi left a trail of evidence on his computer that was in danger of being compromised. For both our sakes, it needed to be destroyed."

"And Kenny?"

"He's not the first mistake I've made in hiring people. I was counting on him to be as level-headed and goal-focused as his father. He let his ego and his temper get in the way."

"So I'll ask again—should I be worried?"

"Only you can answer that. You know what my expectations are."

They sat in the black-haired partner's office. Though this room had real furniture, it wasn't that much cleaner than the unfinished rooms they'd been forced to abandon on the thirteenth floor. Sniffling at the dust provided a legitimate reason to dab the nose with a handkerchief to mask the room's working-class smell. And he expected them to sip coffee like civilized people?

The man sitting across the desk had no trouble downing the thick brew. "I don't like changing things when we're this close to getting what we want. It makes me nervous." He set his mug down on a messy stack of papers, his dark eyes wide as a lightbulb went on inside. "You were planning to take him out all along, weren't you? That's cold."

Hmm. Maybe he wasn't such a malleable idiot, after all. "I took no pleasure in killing the boy."

There'd been no regret, either. It was simply a matter of doing what had to be done.

There was little in life that evoked any kind of emotional response these days, except for obsession with the plan. The plan was everything. What was the old adage? Living well is the best revenge? Eventually they'd get there. The opportunity to live very, very well had been the key motivator to recruit the experts needed for each specific task.

But creating and carrying out the plan itself— besting the brilliant Damon Sinclair—was the real prize. It was the main reason to get up in the morning, the only true satisfaction that life still offered after being cheated out of so much. They'd had an initial setback with the codes and inability to break into Damon Sinclair's lab. But mistakes were easily dealt with. Anyone who stood in the way of the intended outcome—either through incompetence, weak will and a loose tongue, or just plain bad timing—was considered a mistake. It was a basic law of business—trim the fat and hold tight to the goals of the plan.

"Kenny had to go. The boy couldn't keep his mouth shut. And Sinclair and that woman were too close." Standing and stretching reinvigorated a body that had once been in much better shape. "My involvement must remain completely secret or Sinclair will gain the upper hand. And I got tired of his having all the advantage a long time ago."

The black-haired man had the nerve to question their progress. "You think we have an advantage? There's still a chance the old lady could wake up and tell someone she recognized you. Or me."

Back to idiot, after all. If it wasn't that he had one valuable role left to play, he might be gone as well.

"If we're lucky, she'll die of old age before I have to go back and finish the job. In the meantime, the good doctor seems to have a new weakness." Outside the window, the streetlights glinted off the sleek finish of Damon Sinclair's black Lexus as it pulled into the parking garage next door. The woman in the front seat with him was chatting away, as usual. Was that a nervous habit? Or did she really think she had something interesting to say?

"I've seen what you mean." The black-haired man came to the window as well. "Who'd have thought she could be his type? Brassy, bossy. No style beyond plain and simple. Hell, I bet she doesn't even own a dress."

"A man gets lonely. Besides, all he feels for her is guilt. Responsibility. That has always been a downfall of Dr. Sinclair's—thinking he has to take care of others because he's so much smarter or richer than any of them. Such arrogance. He pours his cash into this money pit for a handful of tenants who barely exist."

"I thought buying the building was your idea. To get him away from the main offices and security force at SinPharm."

True. Having Sinclair working off-site had given them both the access and cover to plant the original "accidental" explosion in his lab. But that had not gone as smoothly as originally envisioned.

Now the headache was back, throbbing between the eyes and at the rear of the skull. "I meant it to be a short-term investment for resale. I had no idea he'd get caught up in historical reclamation." Massaging the back of the neck did nothing to ease the pain. "He gives patients their medications for free or at reduced rates. Spends millions on research for the 'benefit of humanity'…and he doesn't even take care of his own. Except for that old woman." Bank accounts didn't lie. "He let the profit margin slide, and company revenues went down."

"I thought you said he took the hit himself so that investors wouldn't see any of that loss."

"All his top executives took that hit. But he was the only one who could really afford it. If he'd listened to me, and reinvested instead of giving and spending, we'd all be rich." And none of this would have had to happen. "He has a head for science, not business. That's why he's always needed me. That's why he'll wish he'd listened to my advice when he had the chance."

Jock Hannity should have listened. Kenny Kenichi should have listened.

"He'll listen now. Or lose everything. He will give us those codes and he will pay. For costing me a fortune I have every right to, and for what he did to Miranda Sinclair."

The black-haired man went pensive. "I loved her, you know. I miss her."

"I know." It didn't mean anything, but the beard-roughened face deserved a gentle touch. "In her own way, I think she loved you, too." *Now where's my handkerchief?* The hand needed to be wiped clean. "But she's gone."

The black-haired man had never liked that answer. "So why was Kenny the only casualty when you had a chance to take out Sinclair *and* that Snow woman at the same time?"

"Because that wasn't the plan." Damon Sinclair hadn't suffered enough. "The doctor and the woman will die. But on my terms, not because it's convenient."

"And the money?"

"Don't get ahead of yourself. Everything is in place now." A pointed look demanded absolute success. "If you did your job as I instructed."

The black-haired man laid a rough hand on his partner's shoulder and squeezed. Once upon a time, a massage like that had been service enough.

But his next words gave even more pleasure.

"It's done. All of it. All you have to do is tell me when. Then that lab, and all of its secrets, will be ours."

Did the idiot really not have any idea how this was going to play out? *I guess broad shoulders and technical know-how only get you so far.*

The Sinclair lab and all of its secrets will be mine.

Chapter Ten

"Good night, tough guy."

Kit leaned down and kissed Matt's cheek before pulling the covers up around his shoulders. Sprawled across the sofa bed in Damon's book-lined study, he looked more like the baby brother who'd made a regular habit of tucking plastic bugs into her pockets or beneath her pillow, just to hear her scream. She smoothed Matt's hair off his forehead, feeling a stab of unexpected grief when she saw that without the spiky hair and attitude, he was growing into a carbon copy of their father.

"Keep an eye on this one, Dad," she prayed. "Keep him safe."

Gritting her teeth to keep the sentimental tears in check, Kit cinched her robe tight around her waist and headed for the crack of light at the door. She'd sat there in the shadows, watching Matt sleep, long after they'd finished their heart-to-heart and he'd drifted off to sleep. They hadn't resolved every issue between them, but the lines of communication were open and a couple of basic agreements had been made. One, she'd be less of an overprotective second mom and more of a friend if he was less secretive and gave her fewer reasons to worry. And two, they loved each other. They shared a bond forged by a happy childhood and tested by grief and danger. That bond would hold, no matter what other challenges life threw their way.

But she'd silently mused on the past long enough. Time to take care of the needs of the present. Inhaling a deep, fortifying breath, Kit silently closed the door behind her and went in search of their host.

The bedroom loft on the second level was dark, and she hadn't heard Damon go up the stairs so she doubted he was asleep. The kitchen and living room were empty, the bathrooms unoccupied.

"Damon?" Her voice echoed off the tall windows and granite-and-steel decor, reinforcing the isolation she felt. If she could get this lonely chill after only a couple of hours in the penthouse, how must Damon feel living here 24/7? Compassion twisted in her heart and made Kit even more determined to track down where he might have gone.

She paused in the kitchen to pour two glasses of milk, hoping a little bit of noisy activity would

capture his attention. Had the man gone somewhere without telling her? To visit Helen at the
hospital, perhaps? Was he out in the night, lurking
in the shadows, waiting to rescue someone else
whose life was in danger? Or was she the only
troublesome neighbor on that unique to-do list?

Curiouser and curiouser.

If she could find Henry Phipps with thirty
stories of the Sinclair Tower to search, she could
find Damon Sinclair on the top two floors.
Padding along the hallway in her stocking feet, Kit
carried the two glasses toward the private rooms
where Helen lived, and where Damon had instructed her to make herself at home for the night.

Helen's room held nothing but Kit's own discarded clothes. The bathroom was empty, a small
reading room was dark. "Damon?" She knocked
on a door across the hall and discovered a pantry
filled with food stores and cleaning supplies. But
no scientist. "Hmm. Maybe you do materialize
and vanish out of thin air."

Not likely. What was she missing here? Another
secret passageway like the one on the thirteenth
floor? But she could find no hidden archways, no
suspicious velvet drapes.

Kit wandered on down the hall to the steel door
at the end marked Fire Exit. Dead end? She
stopped and drank her milk and considered what
she knew about the man. Not much, beyond

having an aversion to people and a diehard need to pay off any debt he felt he owed. He had a brilliant mind, a penchant for secrets, a seductive voice that matched the shadows he loved so well, scarred-up hands and that moon-kissed hair.

And he radiated a clean, masculine scent that reminded her of sex and science and…

Kit sniffed the air. "That scent."

A familiar awareness stirred inside her, making her itchy inside her skin. Damon had been here. Recently or often, or both. Had he paced the hallway near Helen's rooms, worrying about the grandmotherly figure since her attack?

Or…

Kit polished off her milk and tucked the empty glass beneath her arm. Then she braced her hand against the crossbar on the door. This was either another one of Damon's secrets or… "You're going to be really ticked when I open this and all the building alarms go off."

Kit squinched her face together and pushed.

CLICK.

She cracked one eye open. No alarm.

She opened both eyes and stared out onto the landing of a black steel staircase that doubled back on itself and descended into the darkness beneath her feet.

"Damon Sinclair, man of mystery." She was at

once intrigued and rightly cautious about the man's eccentricities. She stepped out onto the steel grating and ran her fingers along the railing. Unlike the passageway on the thirteenth floor, this stairwell was clean—spotlessly so—indicating regular use. But who dusted a fire escape? "Hello?"

Kit called into the darkness without really expecting a response. She felt along the wall for a light switch, but found none. She supposed a man with Damon's keen sense of perception didn't need a light to find his way through the shadows. He'd proved that at the hospital, and earlier tonight at the Black Hole Café.

"Damon? Are you down there?" She was already on the third step before she paused to rationalize why she was investigating shadows. Something more than curiosity drew her toward the most secret of places in Damon Sinclair's dark domain.

There were certain things they needed to discuss before either of them turned in. Like, what did he and Matt discuss while she'd been in the shower earlier? Was he going to press charges against her brother for testing his computer skills on SinPharm's database? Did Damon have any idea who would want Kenny Kenichi dead? Did he think the same person would come after Matt now? Clearly he believed there was some sort of danger, or he wouldn't have insisted they stay the night within the extra security of his penthouse. Did he think the attempts on her life and Helen's were related to Kenny's efforts to hack his way into Damon's private work files?

And why the hell was it so wrong for them to kiss each other when he'd gone out of his way to hold her hand—to hold her—as though there was something very personal going on between them?

Finding the answer to any one of those questions justified the risk of following the hidden staircase to see if it led her to Damon. Besides, it would be rude to close herself off in Helen's room without even saying thank you and good night.

Either her eyes were getting as adept at seeing in the dark as Damon's were, or there really was a light shining at the bottom of the stairs, casting a dim glow through the metal gratings beneath her feet. She curled her toes into each step, trying to decide whether descending into the unknown would be as wise a move for her as it was for the foolish heroines who populated horror movies. "As long as I don't fall down if I have to run away," she reasoned out loud, buying some courage with a stab at humor.

By the time she reached the second landing, the light had taken shape and grown brighter, drawing Kit like a beacon. There was a door down there, made of glass and steel. The light shining through it seemed artificially bright in the pall of the stairwell. But as Kit reached it, she could see the treasure hidden inside the room—tables, lab equipment, a bank of computers, a row of monitors suspended from the ceiling, walls lined with white boards that had mathematical equations and chemical diagrams sketched across them in a powerful scrawling hand.

It had been more than a year since Kit had seen the inside of a laboratory, and she'd never been inside one this complex and completely stocked with the latest equipment. The goodies inside that lab were more exciting to her than a dozen roses from the most ardent suitor would be to any other woman.

"Wow." She braced her hand against the door's steel frame and peered through the window. She could bet this state-of-the-art retreat didn't show up on any public blueprint of the Sinclair Tower. This was where the great Dr. Damon Sinclair created his miracles. This must have been the site of the explosion and fire that had cost him his eye and eventually his wife. But nothing inside looked damaged now.

Except, perhaps, for the tall, lean man hunched over a table set with three different microscopes at the far side of the room.

The lab coat he wore hugged his broad shoulders like a second skin and created a stark contrast against his black turtleneck. But it wasn't the bleak fashion choice or even the taut strap of his eyepatch cutting a dark stripe across the back of his silver-blond hair that made Kit catch her breath with a mix of trepidation and concern.

It was the blood staining the cuff of his left sleeve.

What was he doing in there?

"You really are a mad scientist." She mouthed the words, bathing the glass in the fog of her breath.

As soon as she whispered, Damon stilled. His shoulders tensed and his jaw angled to the side, as though he'd sensed her presence. Kit quickly wiped the glass clean with the sleeve of her robe and retreated to the base of the stairs. But there was nowhere to run from the piercing scrutiny of that deep-blue eye as he turned and spotted her. No place to hide as he rose and strode across the length of the room.

There was nothing more compelling than the sight of all that focused intensity bearing down on her with such purpose.

Kit swallowed hard and held tight to the metal railing. Her breath came in a stuttered gasp. And for one foolish moment, something feral and feminine and too long neglected awakened inside her. She wanted Damon Sinclair. Wanted more than his protection, more than a thank-you check. She wanted his brain, his body, wanted whatever heart he had left inside him.

She wanted him to want her in that same crazy, inexplicable way that was tearing at her soul.

Oh, man, she'd made some pretty bold choices in her lifetime. But falling for Damon Sinclair, trusting him despite his eccentricities, wanting a man who'd made it clear that he would never confuse sexual chemistry with something emotional was crazy. Plum crazy. Maybe *she* was the mad one here.

Damon pressed a button and the door slid open. A wave of cold air from inside the lab washed over her like a bucket of reviving water. She had to think here, not just…want.

Kit summoned a friendly smile. "This setup is totally amazi—"

"What the hell are you doing here?"

The scowl on his expression might have made a different woman turn tail and run back up the stairs. But Kit only knew a perverse urge to touch his mouth to see if she could coax the grim line into a smile. "That's the second time you've greeted me that way. A girl could get a complex."

"Is something wrong?" He took another step closer, filling the doorway, silhouetting his face and shoulders, forcing her to imagine that his expression matched the urgent concern in his voice. "Is there a problem with Matt?"

"No. He's zonked upstairs."

"Then go to bed."

"I'm too keyed up to sleep." Even though she'd showered and changed into her flannel pajamas and robe, Damon was still fully dressed in the same dark jeans and fitted sweater he'd been wearing at the Black Hole. She wasn't the only night owl up prowling the hidden recesses of the Sinclair Tower. "I thought you might like some company."

"I'm working."

"At two in the morning?" A moment's hesitation made her wonder if he was rethinking his Garbo-esque claims for wanting to be alone. And when he didn't actually tell her to go away again, Kit seized the advantage. She closed the distance between them and pushed the glass of milk into his hand. "I thought you might want something to drink, to help you decompress after all the excitement tonight. Besides, the carton was almost empty and I didn't want it to sour on you. I can run downstairs and get some milk from the diner in the morning."

Up close, she could see him studying the glass in his hand as though either the milk or the kindness was a foreign concept to him. When Kit felt his gaze shift to her, she had the idea that *she* might be the foreign concept to him.

"You really need to go to the grocery store. Or is that something Helen does for you so you don't have to go out? Of course, you've been going out a lot more lately because of…well, we don't really seem to know who's behind these scrapes I keep getting into, do we?" The moment that remembered fear crept into her consciousness, Kit quickly changed the subject. "This level isn't accessible from the public stairwell or the elevators, is it?"

Chatty, curious neighbor, standing in the semi-darkness outside a hidden laboratory? Definitely a foreign concept, judging by the way he watched her like a specimen beneath a microscope.

"How did you find me?"

"Deductive reasoning. I didn't hear you leave the penthouse, but you weren't anyplace I could see, so you had to be someplace I couldn't see." She grinned as she tried to peek around him into the lab. But those shoulders and attitude guarded the entrance and kept her at bay. "May I come in?"

"You don't belong here."

"Mr. Kronemeyer warned me that I should stay off the upper floors of the building. Is this why? So no one discovers your private lab?"

The blue eye narrowed. "The crew before Kronemeyer's built this lab to my specifications. He doesn't know anything about this place. He's got no business threatening you."

So the guard dog's hackles were up on her behalf. Damon's protection was comforting—but not quite the relationship she wanted with her intriguing neighbor.

"Kronemeyer's just a grumpy butt who works and worries too much." She waved aside the fear and anger she'd felt when he'd forced her off the thirteenth floor. "So what are you working on now?"

"Getting rid of you." He raised the glass to his lips, taking the sting out of his gruff answer.

Kit laughed. "Careful, Doc. Somebody might find out that the only thing you're hiding up here is your sense of humor."

"I am not one of your community projects. You can't fix me."

"Do you need to be fixed?"

"Don't."

The deep-pitched word fell into the shadows around them, filling the quiet with an edgy awareness that chased away teasing humor and pricked goose bumps across the back of Kit's neck. "Don't try to help you? Or don't care that you're hurting?" She nodded toward the smears on his cuff. "By the way, you're bleeding again."

He returned the glass and backed her toward the stairs. "Good night."

When he turned away, assuming she'd meekly follow his edict and march back up the stairs, Kit slipped past him. She brushed against his heat and strength and darted beyond his outstretched hand into the center of the lab.

"Kit." She heard his footsteps in quick pursuit. "Dammit, woman, you don't belong here."

She took in every piece of equipment she could identify, and made note of the ones she couldn't. A quick read of the walls revealed prospective formulas that were both carbon- and silicon-based. She ducked around a table to escape his reach and get a look at the familiar images on the television monitors. The street in front of the diner. The darkened lobby. The elevator and hall-way at Damon's penthouse door.

Kit didn't know whether to admire the thoroughness of his security setup or be offended. "So, you're not superhuman, after all. Instead of taking part in the world, you watch it on TV. You knew when to come to the rescue because you're spying on me. On everything in the building." She glanced over her shoulder at the glare closing in on her. "Is that legal?"

"It's state-of-the-art security. With two fires, all the accidents and this equipment… Hell, I don't have to explain anything to you." He grabbed hold of her arm, but something about the blood-soaked gauze on his left hand lying against the soft pink of her sleeve seemed to disgust him. He jerked his hand back and cursed, giving Kit the opportunity to slide across the room.

"Have you ever seen me, uh…?" She pulled at the top button of her pajama top.

"No. It only accesses public venues." He crossed to a table littered with first-aid supplies and snatched up a cloth towel to wrap around his knuckles.

"So you had a view of Helen's attack." She set down the milk glasses when she found the keyboard controlling the monitors, and pressed the arrow keys, testing how to adjust the camera shots. "Did you see where Old Henry went on one of these things?"

"Stop that." Long fingers wound around her wrist and pulled her toward the exit, forcing her into double-time to keep up with Damon's demanding stride. "I don't know what happened to your friend. And I fell asleep the night Helen was assaulted. Otherwise, those men would have already been dealt with." The threat in his voice gave way to the same helpless frustration she felt. "Trust me, I've studied that tape, frame by frame, trying to get a face or clue to tell me who hurt her."

The same frames replayed themselves in Kit's memory. "It wouldn't do you any good. They wore stocking masks."

"Like the so-called nurse who attacked you at

the hospital?" Damon halted his manic effort to herd her out of the lab. The stop was so abrupt that Kit plowed into the wall of his back. But he pushed her away before his heat and hardness and addictive scent could do more than register on her feminine radar. "You said he had no face."

He squeezed her shoulder, demanding she tip her chin and meet his gaze.

"Right. I remember it now." The same red mask with white circles around the eyes. Only, the hair that poked through at the hospital had been blond, not black like the man who'd hurt Helen. "He wasn't as big as the man in the alley. I mean, he was taller than me, but not bulky. I wonder if describing the mask to a sketch artist would help the police with their investigation."

The grip on her wrist eased. Maybe she imagined the thumb stroking against her pulse. "Was it the same mask?"

"Same style."

"Probably something fairly common."

Kit nodded. *We're all dead.* The intonation of Helen's last words before losing consciousness played through Kit's memory. Damon cursed and pulled away, leaving Kit fidgeting with frustration. She wondered how much stemmed from the ugly memory and how much was the direct result of losing contact with Damon's warmth.

Comfort and support had been denied. Had she

really expected him to care? Or was that just more of that foolish wanting?

She raked her fingers through her hair and slowly turned to study every corner of the lab—from the petri dish beneath the microscope beside her to the card and keypad security lock at either exit. *Think, Kit. Piece it together. Help this all make sense.* She looked back at the security lock. "Did Helen know about this lab?"

"Yes." Damon was trying to tie the towel ends together to keep it in place. He was using his right hand, his teeth and a tricky balancing act. "She'd bring me a meal from time to time. Come down to check on me if I didn't show up for breakfast."

"Does anyone else know this is here?"

"The men who built it. They were contracted through SinPharm, then bonded to secrecy."

"Through SinPharm," she echoed. "That means Easting Davitz knows, right? He represents you at Sinclair Pharmaceuticals—he's your front man. He knows about this lab, doesn't he?"

Damon cursed at the towel, pulled it from the wound and tossed it across the table. "Easting is like a second father to me. He wouldn't hurt the company or Helen."

"Need some help?" Kit went to pick up the towel and discovered a much bigger problem. Clearly, Damon had tried to tend his own wound, without much success. She separated soiled gauze and cotton from the clean supplies, then spotted a sink and went to wash her hands. "Does he know how to get in here?"

"I'm a doctor. I can manage my own injury." *As if.* "And the answer's no. Getting in requires a key card and a variable access code. Easting doesn't have either one."

"Helen does." Those thugs really were just trying to steal her keys. Only the key Helen carried could unlock millions of dollars' worth of secrets. "If she brings you a meal 'from time to time,' she knows how to get in here." Kit dried her hands and filled a clean beaker with water. She paid closer attention to the experiments lining the room as she returned to the table. "They're using her to get to your secrets."

Damon sank onto a nearby stool as the color drained from his face. Kit rushed to his side, thinking blood loss had finally beaten his will to go on. But as she braced a hand at his shoulder and biceps to steady him, she could see it was one of those dreaded emotions, not any physical weakness that assailed him. "They left her for dead, just to get the damn key?" He pounded his fist against the table, scattering the items on the table and jolting Kit inside her socks. "Bastards. The key card doesn't work unless they punch in the code. They hurt her for nothing!"

His pain was evident in the tight line of his mouth that hovered right before her eyes. Kit risked staying put, wondering if she dared offer anything as mundane as a hug. Or if he'd even welcome such comfort. In the end she soothed the beast by simply gentling her voice. "Are you talking about a code like the one Kenny and Matt were trying to break?"

"No, that's for something different. I encrypt all my work. With the right translation, someone could recreate my equations. Produce the Sin-Pharm formulas themselves. They could make a fortune selling them to a competitor and put me out of business."

"A code for this, a code for that—you're a little paranoid, aren't you?"

He shrugged her hand off his shoulder. "It's time for you to leave."

"Not when we're about to figure this out. Not when you need me."

Damon shot to his feet, towering over her. "*We* are not about to do anything. And I do not need…"

His gaze on her shoulder drew her own focus to the drop of blood that stained her robe.

The tortured guilt that haunted his expression made it impossible not to reach out to him. Kit stroked a fingertip across the square line of his stubbled jaw. "I'm okay, Damon. I'm not hurt."

She summoned a reassuring smile. "You didn't hurt me."

"I will, though. I lost Miranda. Helen nearly died. And you…" He hooked a finger around a strand of hair that had caught at the corner of her mouth and pulled it free. He tucked it behind her ear and let his fingertip mirror her gentle touch on him. "You nearly died. *Stick with me, baby.*" Sarcasm sounded particularly poignant in his rusty tone. "The people around me pay a horrible price for getting involved with me."

Kit caught his hand in hers and offered her strength. "Let's just focus on the present, okay? Don't worry about what might happen a few minutes or a few days from now. Just be with me. Here. Now." She splayed her fingers at the center of his chest and nudged him back onto the stool. "I saw that you wouldn't let the paramedics treat your hand back at the Black Hole. I won't let you off that easily."

"You're a warrior, aren't you." His gruff expression eased into a wry smile. "You don't back down from anything. Not even a son of a bitch like me."

"You have your moments." Kit cradled his injured hand between both of hers and moved it into the bright light that shone down on the table. "I think I'm half-afraid that if I ever turn away from the things that frighten me or hurt me—and start running—that I'll never be able to stop. When my folks died, I knew I had to be strong for Matt. Germane depended on Mom and Dad, too. And the neighborhood depended on the diner…" She peeled off the old bandage. "Running scared just isn't an option for me."

"Do *I* frighten you?"

Once, maybe. While she didn't agree with his choice, she thought she could understand why he isolated himself and clung to the darkness— Henry's addled terror when Damon had busted into the squatter's apartment to rescue her, the screams from the waitress at the Black Hole, the paramedics' awkward hesitance at seeing the deforming scars and ridges on Damon's hand. Riled up, half-hidden in shadow, Damon Sinclair easily startled, and often frightened the faint of heart.

But she saw something more. The intelligence shining in that piercing blue eye. The seductive slant of those male lips. The spirit of a man willing to put his life on the line to protect her.

"Kit?" he prompted, his dark, husky voice sending a skitter of intimate awareness down her spine.

She soaked a gauze pad in the water and began cleaning the bullet graze that grooved his palm and the inside of his fingers. "I think what frightens me are the things I feel when I'm around you."

"And what do you feel?"

Tending Damon's wound was a little like petting a big jungle cat. He sat and let her spread the antibiotic ointment that would help prevent infection, but Kit got the feeling that he was all coiled energy, more aware of his surroundings—and of her—than she could imagine. One wrong word, one false move, and the panther would pounce and she would be at his mercy.

But for now she was the one in control. Her soft words and gentle touches seemed to have a mesmerizing effect on the cat. And his radiant warmth and hushed talking in that low-pitched growl seemed to have an equally mesmerizing effect on her.

She'd make easy prey if he chose to turn on her now.

"I feel…" How could she explain the soul-deep connection she felt to this man when she could barely understand it herself? There were so many things that separated him from the rest of the world—his fearsome appearance, his intellect, his money, his secretive moods. But she felt an affinity for him in every touch, every conversation, every look—he stimulated her brain, aroused her body and touched her heart. *Yeah, right.* Try explaining that ethereal notion to a man of science.

"I feel like I'm…" She tried to laugh off the deep turn her thoughts had taken. "Well, you'd sure be easier to hang around with if you were some mild-mannered accountant or regular Joe."

"You'd be better off with a regular Joe." He dutifully turned his hand so she could clean and dry the back. "He might actually ask you out on a date. Take you to a museum or research center where you could indulge that curiosity of yours. At least he'd meet you in the daytime. Maybe even outside. In the light."

"You're not a vampire. You're just a night owl, like me. Only, you take it to the extreme. I'm guessing it's easier to avoid people and their reactions that way. Though, to give the rest of us credit, we all have hang-ups of one kind or another. Yours are just…obvious." She'd guess that building and working in a secret laboratory wasn't all about professional security. This was his sanctuary. The big cat's lair. This was probably the one place he could completely relax. But Kit didn't voice that opinion. Instead, she frowned and raised his hand for a closer look at his fingers. "That's odd."

"I lost some of my fingerprints in the fire," he explained, misunderstanding her interest.

But that wasn't what had caught her eye. The wound from Kenny's bullet bisected the webwork of scars and keloids that covered his hands. But that wasn't what she'd noticed, either. "You have new skin—new scars—growing across the wound already."

The panther cat had had enough. Damon curled his fingers into his palm and stood. "Good night, Kit."

She caught his sleeve and held on as he shoved the stool back. "Don't pull away. Explain it to me."

"Ever the curious one, aren't you?"

"Is that your tissue regeneration formula at work? Did you inject yourself with something?"

"Years ago." He turned his hands, palms up, palms down, looking at them with contempt. "I cut my hand in the lab one day. Thought it'd be a smart idea to test the formula on myself. It worked, all right. Every paper cut, every splinter I've had since has repaired itself. The cells in my hands were reprogrammed to expel any foreign object and regrow the damaged tissue. They've been doing their job ever since. I haven't yet figured how to reverse it." He held up his hands as though a good look would scare her away. "These scars aren't from the fire—they're from the healing."

But Kit could only see the miracle at work. "So, you weren't worried about Kenny shooting you in the hand because you knew you could heal yourself?" Her lips parted in wonder as she took one hand and inspected the reconstructive work more carefully. "That's bloody brilliant, Doc. It's as if microscopic nanites are replacing the tissue, cell by cell."

"It's not quite that sci-fi." He offered only token resistance when she resumed the first aid. Maybe he just wanted to get the scars hidden as quickly as possible. Or maybe, just maybe, she was wearing down a few of those distant emotional walls he wore like protective armor. "I perfected a later version—the one that was patented and put on the public market. It doesn't stay in the system and alter it permanently."

She wrapped gauze around the wound and taped it to the back of his hand. "Will the stuff that was injected into me have any long-term effects?"

"I don't think so. That's one reason I..." His gaze slid over to the row of microscopes. "I've been examining your blood work and tissue samples. Running some tests on them."

Kit gathered up the trash and tossed it on her way to examine what was beneath the lens in the first microscope. "K26," she read on the slide label. She looked at the rapidly growing cells. "Is this me?" Kit's stomach flip-flopped with an unsettled feeling—either this was really weird, or Damon was showing his concern in the only way he knew how. "I'm a science experiment?"

"No." She felt his heat beside her and lifted her

head to see the earnest hesitation in his expression. "I think..." He reached out and stroked her jaw, petting her. Apologizing? "I think there's something unique about your genetic makeup. When you rejected the 428 formula, I suspected. Now I'm sure."

"Of what?"

His fingers slipped into her hair as he cupped her jaw in his palm. "That you're a miracle."

Kit's stomach flip-flopped for a completely different reason. "Me?"

"It's still in the rudimentary stages, not anywhere near ready for testing on live subjects or taking to market, but in the past, my formulas haven't worked on people who share the same allergies you do."

If his words weren't so darn clinical, she'd think he was sweet-talking her. Who was she kidding? With the way she loved science, he was seducing her with that tone and that gentle touch. "But you found something in my genes that makes the formulas work?"

"Yes."

Had he stepped closer? Or was the temperature in the lab rising? She reached up and wrapped a steadying hand around his wrist. "So is *K26* named after me?"

His other hand, his bandaged hand, came up to brush another wayward tendril off her cheek.

"It's not quite so romantic as naming a rose after you, but—"

Kit pressed two fingers to his lips to silence the apology. "I'm flattered. Something you created from me may help save lives. I'm sure that makes me weird, but I think that's cool."

"Thank you." His lips moved beneath her sensitive fingertips, creating dozens of erotic sparks that zipped along each nerve and tingled in the tips of her breasts and at the heart of her. "There's nothing weird about you, Kit. Unless you count this willingness to let me touch you."

"Damon—"

"Shh. I surrender. I keep trying to keep my distance, but you won't let me." Though his words and tone were meant to calm, her pulse started beating faster. "Your freckles are cool to the touch. Which is a neat trick, considering the fire inside you. Your hair is like amber silk. And, unless you stop me…" He *was* moving closer. "I'm going to conduct a little scientific observation."

His warm breath danced across her lips. "What's that?"

"I want to know if you taste as soft and warm and amazing as you look."

His lips closed over hers in a tender exploration. Kit's lips parted and his gasp mingled with her own. His catlike tongue moved inside and slid against her own. Kit reached up to wrap her fingers around his other wrist, needing to hold on with two hands as her knees went weak.

He suckled her bottom lip between his. "Soft," he observed.

He nipped down gently and Kit trembled in response. "Warm."

His fingers tunneled into her hair and tilted her head back to open her mouth more fully beneath his. "Amazing."

The pressure grew more demanding as he turned her and backed her into the table. His hips crowded against hers, and one muscular thigh wedged its way between her own. Kit shivered at the friction between rough denim and soft flannel. She moaned at the contrast of hard muscle pressing against her soft heat.

"Damon—" Did that helpless plea come from her own throat?

"As amazing as I remember."

No. *Better.*

Kit abandoned her grip on his wrists and splayed her fingers across the flat of his stomach. The catch of his breath beneath her touch was an exhilarating, empowering thing. The jungle cat was letting her play. The nubby ribs of his sweater tickled her palms, but it wasn't enough. She boldly dragged her palms to his waist and flanks, loving every hitch of muscle and catch of breath.

She found the hem of his sweater, then slipped her hands beneath and singed herself on hot, taut skin.

The cry in her throat drew his lips there. His stubbly beard abraded the soft skin. His lips and tongue soothed it.

He skimmed his hands down her back, pulled her away from the table. He cupped her bottom in two sure hands. Squeezed. Aroused. Lifted.

Then she was sitting on the table. Damon spread her legs and walked between them. Her robe was untied. Off her shoulders. He nibbled an ear, sampled a cord of her neck, gently kissed the fading bruise at her collarbone.

His knuckles brushed against her breasts, elicited shivers of delight as he unhooked the buttons of her shirt and exposed her to his hungry gaze. He cradled the heavy globes in his big, scarred hands, teased the nipples into a hard salute. Then he bent his head to capture a distended peak in his mouth and Kit lurched against him. She dug her fingers into the skin at his waist and threw her head back, losing herself in the powerful need of each touch, each nip, each kiss.

Kit felt heavy inside. Molten. Alive.

She was no big sister. No short-order cook. No orphan or failed grad student. No nosy friend or neighborhood guardian. She was a woman. Distilled into her purest, most feminine form. And the man laying claim to her had taken her to that place.

"Damon. Please." She needed his kiss. Needed his strength. Needed him.

"I want you," he growled against her mouth. The unspoken evidence was already swelling behind his jeans and pressing against her thigh. "I shouldn't. But I do."

She scraped her palms along the smooth cut of his hair and angled his mouth back to hers. "I want you, too."

"It's been so long." He stole a kiss. "I don't know if I can make this last." He slipped a hand inside her shirt and squeezed her breast. "Don't know if I can make it good."

"The only way—" Kit swept the lab coat off his shoulders, tempted him with another kiss before tugging at the hem of his sweater and helping him remove it "—it won't be good…" He returned the favor. She was naked down to her waist. The cold air of the lab teased her skin but couldn't find its way inside to rob her of this erupting heat. "…is if you stop."

He scooped a hand beneath her bottom, circled his arm behind her back. He picked her up against him, binding them body to body, skin to skin, trust to trust and, in some very elemental way, soul to soul.

Kit wrapped her arms around his neck and held

on as her pajama pants disappeared and his jeans and shorts dropped to the floor. When he sat her back on the table and entered her, Kit nearly exploded, right on the spot.

Oh, yeah. Damon's experiment was a raging success.

And neither one of them was stopping.

Chapter Eleven

For the first time in months, Damon considered opening the two-story blinds that shaded the windows on the east side of the penthouse and letting the morning sun pour in.

But that would require getting out of bed, going downstairs and pressing the button that operated the window coverings. And he didn't want to do anything to spoil the moment of waking up with Katherine Elizabeth Snow's naked body snuggled against his chest.

Her soft breathing warmed a spot near the base of his neck, and her bare, palm-size breast pressed against his side was shamelessly warming up a spot farther down on his body. She dozed peacefully, no doubt worn-out by the demands he'd made and the passion she'd so willingly shared. First, in his lab, where the intensity of their need had made up for his lack of seductive finesse. And then again in the loft, where he'd remembered a condom and tried to slow things down and do it right for her. Though, when Kit had urged him onto his back and straddled him, ideas of finesse disappeared and he'd been as eager to take her as she'd been to receive him.

Maybe it was that third time, just before dawn, when he realized just how quickly he was falling in love with this woman.

Damon had been seized by the nightmares again. Thrashing in his sleep, caught up in the fires that wanted to destroy everything he cared about. Kit's firm voice and firmer touch had reached him in the fiery darkness, and he'd awakened to the glorious, Renaissance-painting-worthy sight of the moonlight glimmering over her naked breasts and shoulders.

When she knew he was with her again, she'd cradled his head to the pillow of her breasts. She'd held him tight as he latched on to her and shared the haunting tales from his dreams. She hadn't recoiled when he'd removed the eyepatch and tried to explain how the glass eye was uncomfortable and needed to be adjusted, but since no one ever saw him, anyway, what did it matter?

She'd kissed him above his eye, massaged the tender skin at his temples, soothed him with gentle words.

And when he'd pulled her down beneath him and entered her that third time, she'd opened herself and welcomed him in a way that was more healing than any miracle cure he could devise. He'd been alone for so long; he hadn't let himself feel or care. He hadn't known how desperately he needed the kind of acceptance she offered him. Acceptance as a man—not a scientist, not a prodigy, not a provider. Through her eyes he wasn't the monster he thought he'd become. But then, she'd given him that long ago when her curiosity had overridden any natural aversion to his appearance. She'd given him that with her fearless determination to question him, argue with him—treat him like a normal man.

Kit Snow had given him a gift far greater than saving the life of his dear Helen. Greater than the tender ministrations with which she'd doctored his hand.

Her caring had cracked open the prison inside him and given him back his heart.

He dipped his head and pressed a kiss to the silky crown of her hair. "Thank you."

Damon rolled flat on his back and stretched out, wondering if the sun would feel as warm and natural on his face as Kit's body felt nestled against him.

But as he turned his head farther to glance at the clock, the first twinge of discontentment set in. He picked up the eyepatch from the bedside table and pulled it back into place around his head. But that couldn't dispel the image staring back at him from the nightstand. "Oh, damn."

The muscles in his body began to tense, one by one. He swiped his palm over a jaw that needed a shave. But the sense of betrayal didn't leave him.

Miranda's clear blue eyes watched him from the anniversary photo beside the bed. The last picture he'd taken of her, from their trip down to the Bahamas. Their marriage had been in trouble then. She hadn't wanted to be that far from the office, hadn't wanted to be gone for an entire week. In fact, they'd come back just after the weekend.

Maybe it was his imagination, but there was something judging him even then in that photograph. The wind had whipped across the beach that day, but Miranda had managed to avoid the surf and the fun. With the sunset behind her on the hotel room balcony, she was a vision of physical beauty. Every long, blond hair was in place, unlike the wild fan of caramel-colored hair teasing his arm and chest this morning. Miranda's coral lips curved in a secretive, Mona Lisa smile that revealed none of the abandon of Kit's easy laugh. Those blue eyes looked at the camera, but they weren't really looking at *him*. They wouldn't look past the handsome facade that had once been his the way Kit saw so deeply inside him now.

Maybe he hadn't been so desperate to save his

wife eighteen months ago in that fire—he'd been desperate to save their marriage and what they'd once shared. Miranda hadn't killed their love the night she took her own life. It had already been dying a slow, sad death for months before that.

It was time to let go of the guilt and try to remember the love. It was time to let go of the past. Like Kit had encouraged him last night, he wanted to stay in the present. Here. With her.

He reached out and touched the picture frame. "I miss you, babe." He laid the picture facedown and said goodbye to that chapter of his life.

The emotional reawakening was all too new for him to even try thinking about the future.

"Oh, no." The body beside him stirred.

Damon smiled. "Good morn—"

"Oh, my God." Kit sat up and scooted away, clutching the sheet and comforter up over her breasts. "Is that your wife?"

Damon sat up, alarmed by the stricken look on her face, anxious to reclaim the serenity of waking up together. "It's okay, sweetheart. I was just putting the picture away. I forgot it was there."

Those gray eyes darkened with some unnamed emotion and she raked her fingers through the hair he had so thoroughly mussed the night before. "Do you…? Was I just a…? Did you two ever…here?" She pointed to the bed.

"Kit, calm down." Did she honestly think he'd

bed her as a substitute for the wife he had lost? "I've never had any woman in this bed but you. There's nothing in this room—in this penthouse— that belonged to Miranda."

"Except you." She tugged at the covers, and when they wouldn't cooperate, she covered herself with her arms and slipped out of the bed. She spun around, searching for the clothes he'd carried up in the middle of the night. "I can deal with a lot of stuff. But I can't compete with a ghost."

"Compete?"

She pulled on her panties and jeans, and bent down to retrieve the bra that had fallen to the floor. "I have to get downstairs and get the diner open. Germane will have half the prep work already done by now."

"Katherine." She paused for a moment at the use of her full name. But only a moment. She turned her back to him and continued to dress with a modesty she hadn't shown him last night. Maybe things had gone too far too fast for her. But it made no logical sense for the warmhearted woman who'd welcomed him last night to be turning that cold shoulder to him this morning. Damon tossed back the covers and stood beside the bed. "You're the one who always wants to talk. Let's discuss this."

She turned around, saw his naked body, saw *all*

of him, then blushed and turned away. "I don't think I can talk right now."

Damon cursed and reached for his boxer-briefs. "So you can peel the skin away from *my* wounds, but if I dare try to find out what's bugging you, then I'm the monster again?"

"No." She had her blouse on and halfway buttoned when she turned. The panic had left her posture, but the distance was still there in her eyes. "You're not a monster. Please don't say that. I'm sorry. I just…" She concentrated on the rest of her buttons before continuing. "You loved your wife very much. I can tell you've grieved for her." She picked up her sweater and hugged it to her chest. "I was only thinking in the moment last night. But I don't really believe I thought this through. I mean, Matt's downstairs. I have responsibilities."

Good. She was talking. Damon pulled on his jeans and zipped them, hoping a little less skin—a little less *him*—would relax her further. "We were both a little impulsive last night." Her eyes widened. Okay, a *lot* impulsive. "But this wasn't just a fall-into-bed-and-get-my-rocks-off thing. I haven't been with a woman since my wife's death."

"Great." She pulled the sweater over her head, masking her expression.

Maybe she hadn't heard him right. "I haven't *wanted* to be with a woman since Miranda."

"Miranda, hmm? I saw the photograph. She was very beautiful."

"If you like the cool, sophisticated type."

"Who doesn't?" That particular laugh did nothing to ease his concern. Now she was tucking things in, searching for socks and boots. "I guess I'm a convenient stand-in."

That description angered him. Damon circled the bed. "Did I at any time last night belittle you or make you think you were anything but sexy and desirable? That I didn't want you like hell on fire?"

"Fine. We had sex. It was good."

He took her by the arms and forced her to look him in the eye. "We didn't just have sex, and you know it."

"What I know is that you still have feelings for your wife. *I miss you, babe?*" She echoed his words. Her hands rested against his chest, willing to touch, but not clutching at him, needing him the way she had last night. "Were you thinking about her while you were with me? Or did you just feel like you cheated on her afterward?"

Damon released her. She'd knocked the feet right out from any logical argument by nailing the truth. He *had* known a moment of guilt this morning. But it hadn't lasted. He'd acknowledged it and moved on.

But Kit had already grasped that neither of them

had any idea of what they were moving on to. And apparently she needed a few concrete facts to reassure her. Hell. If he could come up with any, he'd be more than willing to share.

She headed for the stairs and Damon followed. "My wife is dead and gone. You are here and very much alive."

When she hesitated, he stopped two steps above her, keeping her beyond arm's reach. "I have… feelings…that I don't know what to do with, Damon. I care about you, and no, I don't regret what happened. But I can't just…I want…"

"What do you want, Kit? Tell me."

Her shoulders heaved with a mighty sigh before she turned and lifted her gaze to his. The tears that welled in her eyes sucker-punched him in the gut. "Something that doesn't exist in the real world where I have to live." She swiped at the tears before they could fall and headed back down the stairs. "I have to get to work. Matt? C'mon, buddy. Get up. We have to go."

She knocked on the study door and went in before Damon could even find the will to move. "Matt?"

She came back out just as quickly. "Dammit, little brother, you'd better be downstairs."

Kit was out the door. It felt as though she was out of his life even before Damon realized he'd already let her in. "Kit? Kit!"

The whole idea of bringing them to the penthouse was to keep her close, keep an eye on her. Keep her and her brother safe.

But that wasn't the only reason he dashed back up the stairs to throw on the rest of his clothes. Last night in his lab, Damon had been afraid to touch her, afraid that his dark world would snuff the light out of hers. But the passion between them could not be denied. His needs had been met. And by doing so, he'd apparently found a whole new way to destroy her happiness. By wanting Kit. Caring about her. Loving her.

He let that last thought slide without really acknowledging it. This was about Kit. He was bound and determined to give her whatever it was she wanted from him—even if it was distance, time to think things through. Even if she decided he'd be too hard a son of a bitch to deal with day in and day out, and wanted nothing more to do with him.

But she was damn well going to tell him to his face what those *feelings* were she was dealing with. He'd do right by her. Whatever it took to make it right with Kit, it would be done.

WHAT WAS SHE THINKING?

What the hell was she thinking?

Kit fiddled with the buttons on the keypad beside

the penthouse elevator, but without a key card, she couldn't make it work. That left the freight elevator, twenty-nine flights of stairs or swallowing her pride and going back inside the penthouse to ask Damon for a key and the code.

Kit headed for the freight elevator.

She'd been thinking that last night with Damon was some sort of fairy tale. He was the proverbial beast and she was the modern-day beauty—if one didn't go for the cool, sophisticated type—who'd freed him from his nightmares and opened his heart to the idea of love.

But there was no happily-ever-after with a man who was still tied up with thoughts of his dead wife. A man who would risk his life to repay a debt would have no qualms about thanking her with a night like they'd shared. She hadn't wanted his money as a thank-you. And she hadn't wanted a night of intimacy that had gone beyond amazing sex as any kind of payment, either. Oh, she'd wanted last night, all right. But she'd forgotten the whole think-with-your-head thing and had led straight from the heart.

Kit raked her fingers through her hair, disturbing the scent that was uniquely Damon's. The familiar soap and musk made her ache. Oh, God, what had she done?

Her *beast* didn't have a heart to give her. It was

still buried in his wife's grave. And Kit wanted so badly what her parents had shared that she wouldn't settle for anything less.

Of course, that left her with damaged pride, some shaky self-esteem and a battered heart that had foolishly opened up and given Damon everything he needed. Everything she'd wanted to give him. But in return—

"Where are you going?" Damon's gruff voice followed her down the hallway.

She'd been so caught up in wishes and regrets that she hadn't even heard him open his door. "To the freight elevator. It's either that or take the stairs." The air rushed from her lungs in a steadying breath. Kit turned around and headed for the stairwell. "On second thought, I could use the exercise to work you out of my system."

He stopped her with a hand on her arm when she tried to pass him. "Kit."

"Just let me go." She jerked her arm away with more force than she needed.

He held his hand up in surrender. "I know, you need to get to work. But I'm not going to let you leave when you're upset like this."

"Upset?" She wheeled around to face him. "*Upset* is when you're cramming for your final exams and you get a phone call that says both your parents are dead and you have to come home and become a mother to a teenager who doesn't want one. You don't get to say no. You don't have time to mourn or rage at the injustice of two good people being taken from the world. *Upset* is when you've got needy, deserving people looking to you to put a roof over their heads and give them meaningful work to do—even if it means giving up your own dreams."

He was scowling at her now, his expression darkening as she ranted on. Kit swallowed hard and put on the brakes, wisely clamping her mouth shut before every emotion trapped inside her tumbled out.

"Kit, I'm so sorry. I know what it's like to lose someone you love. It's tough when the world expects you to pick up the pieces and go on."

Someone you love. Had Damon really moved on? Could he ever?

"What happened between us last night doesn't upset me," she whispered in a more rational tone, explaining her earlier tirade. She focused on that solitary blue eye that seemed to see so much, but understand so little about what she needed. "I'm embarrassed."

"Embarrassed?" He took a step toward her, but Kit held up her hands and he backed away.

"I'm sorry. Not that it happened, but that I read more into it than I should. I'm not real sophisticated that way, I guess." *Not like Miranda.* She shrugged, regaining control of herself as Damon's posture and expression sank back into that dark, moody place where she'd first known him. She regretted that. But maybe it was safer for her, after all, if she held something back. "Well, I have to get to work. The police should be done with their search of the building. I'll come back later this afternoon to get my things."

He didn't touch her again when she walked past and pressed the call button to summon the freight elevator to the top floor. The gears ground together and the cables groaned with the weight of age and steel.

She felt Damon's heat behind her an instant before his rusty voice grated in tune with the elevator. "Until we know who shot Kenny and tried to kill you and Helen, you're not going anywhere without me."

She shook her head. "You have your research to do. I promise I won't leave the building. You can watch me on one of your monitors."

The elevator arrived at their floor and clicked and moaned to a stop. Damon reached around Kit, unlatched the gate and pushed open the doors. "I'm going with you."

Kit pulled the hem of her sleeves down over her hands and crossed her arms before going inside and standing in the back corner. Damon closed the gate and the doors and pushed the button for the lobby floor before taking a position on the opposite side of the car.

The only sound as the elevator descended was the grind of metal against metal in the gear work above them, and the rumble and shake of the car itself. The silence was strained and awkward. Damon wore his sense of duty in the tight set of his shoulders, and the air between them was heavy with simmering desires and unspoken regrets. With every shake and rattle of the slow descent, Kit huddled tighter in her corner, trying not to think of J. T. Kronemeyer's warning about how the freight elevator needed to be retired, or how much more secure she'd feel with Damon's arms around her.

They were passing the twenty-first floor when she recalled something else J.T. had mentioned. The engineer who was supposed to be fixing the elevators had quit because he heard voices in the elevator shaft.

Either Kit was going nuts, or she was hearing voices, too. It was little more than garbled sounds, but the different tones told her at least two people were engaged in a conversation. Kit's curiosity kicked in, giving her something to focus on besides her feelings for Dr. Brainiac across the way. She looked at the panel of buttons and into every corner for a speaker, but saw nothing. Kit looked up. What if one of the workmen had left a walkie-talkie or cell phone on top of the elevator?

"What is it?" Damon asked. He didn't miss a detail.

"Do you hear that?"

He listened for a moment, then shook his head. "Hear what?"

Kit pushed the button for the twentieth floor and stopped the elevator. "…is the only chance you're going to get. We're on a schedule here. Now get the job done.

"That," she said.

They both held their breath to listen in to more of the fading argument.

"Where's that coming from?" Damon opened the doors and the gate onto the stripped, deserted hallway. Like the thirteenth, it had had no remodeling work done yet. There shouldn't be anyone on the floor. "I don't hear it now."

He shut the gate and doors and pushed a button to resume their descent. Kit heard a different sound, one that seemed to be coming from below them now. She smiled.

"Is that whistling?" Damon asked.

She nodded. "Germane." Something from Earth, Wind and Fire. "There must be something about the open grates of the freight elevator and the acoustics in the shaft that lets us hear sounds all the way from the ground floor."

"And up to the penthouse." The theory made sense. "So we heard a couple of workmen arguing from one of the floors?"

"I guess. The openings in the gate and doors must funnel the sound into the shaft. Germane is probably carrying in deliveries from the loading dock."

She smiled as she eavesdropped on the interrupted tune and heard Matt down there with Germane. They were discussing weekend plans, and Matt was thinking about staying close to home.

Damon heard it, too. "I offered your brother an internship of sorts for the summer—if he keeps his grades up and graduates in May."

"Is that your version of community service for trying to hack into SinPharm?"

"It's good business. I'd like a fresh set of eyes—and ideas—to go through the computer systems and find out just how secure they really are." He slid his gaze across the elevator. "If that's okay with you. It's not any kind of payment you can throw back in my face. Your brother owes me."

Kit agreed. "Sounds like a fair plan. Thank you."

"You're welcome."

Some of the tension between them eased at the

impersonal discussion. Kit almost breathed a sigh of relief.

Instead, her breath lodged in her chest as the air above them erupted with an explosive thunderclap. "What was that?"

"What the hell?"

The elevator shook and jerked to a stop. Kit grabbed the closest railing and found herself wedged between the wall and the shelter of Damon's body. Dust and bits of metal and ceiling foam showered down around them. "Was that—"

"—an explosion."

"Inside the building?" A sick premonition chilled her to the bone, and even the reassuring squeeze of Damon's hand on her shoulder couldn't instill any warmth. "J.T. said he might have to knock out a wall to move some heavy supplies to the top floors."

"That's no construction sound." Damon swung around and pushed the button for the nearest floor, the fifteenth. "We're getting off."

But seconds after he pushed the button, all the lights on the instrument panel flickered and went out. The overhead light followed an instant later.

"Damon?"

He opened the doors, but they were between floors and there was nothing but a steel wall and the greenish cast of emergency lighting to look at. "Damn."

Damon's urgency increased her own. "I don't have my cell phone with me. Do you?"

He shook his head. Of course not. He'd run out of the penthouse to try to catch her. "Stay put."

Like she was going anywhere.

But then she understood. He climbed onto the railing and knocked out one of the ceiling tiles. Then he found something solid to grab hold of and hoisted himself up onto the top of the elevator. "Son of a bitch."

She could only hear what he must be seeing. The awful, yawning groan of bending steel. "Oh, my God." Kit began the pray. "Damon?"

The elevator seemed to sink, like a rubber band slowly stretching out. Only there'd be no bouncing back from this one. The cables would break. The groan of metal became a whipping snap of something taut popping loose. The elevator lurched and Kit grabbed on to the railing.

Damon's long legs reappeared through the opening in the ceiling. He dropped to the floor and the elevator dropped a good six inches before the brakes beneath them screeched to a stop and held. "What's going on?"

Damon reached for her, and she didn't hesitate to cling to his warm, strong hand. "I can't tell from this distance, but I can smell something burning. Up high."

She clung with both hands now. "This isn't just old age or some accident, is it?"

"I don't think so." He tucked her hair behind her ear and spared a moment to cup her jaw and deliver some urgent, silent message she couldn't decipher. "The sixteenth floor's about eight to ten feet above us. We're climbing up and out."

With a nod, Kit stepped into the stirrup of his clasped hands and he boosted her high enough to climb out. Seconds later, he was standing beside her on the roof of the elevator car.

The elevator shifted. Shook. Kit grabbed the center cable for balance, but she could feel it vibrating with the strain of the weight it carried. She could feel it radiating heat as the friction from those vibrations increased.

"Up there?" Eight to ten feet seemed awfully far away. They'd have to stand at the very edge of the elevator's roof, then step across a seemingly bottomless chasm between the car and the wall to even reach the utility ladder. A ladder that looked as though it hadn't been used in years, decades, even. They had to climb up each rickety step to the sixteenth floor, ease onto a narrow ledge, open the gate and crawl out.

"Up there." Damon reached for her hand. "You first. If I lose my grip, I could fall and knock you off the ladder."

She squeezed his hand as she joined him at the edge. "Don't lose your grip."

He was smiling as she took a deep breath and stepped out. "I'll try to catch you if you—"

"I won't fall." She curled her fists around the first narrow rung. It was ice-cold and covered with dust, and when Kit stirred it up, she sneezed. She sniffed away the tickle in her nose and moved her foot to the bottom rung. Bolts scraped against deteriorating concrete, and dust rained down on her head and shoulders. The ladder shook, but it held.

"Go on, sweetheart. You can do it. Don't look down."

Steel creaked. The elevator lurched.

She climbed another rung. "Come on. Get off the elevator."

"The ladder won't hold us both."

Then she had to hurry. Hand over hand, step, push.

Even as she climbed, she heard the voices again. One voice, actually. A tenor's pitch. Cold and deadly and eerily familiar. She knew that voice from the hospital, and from the alley behind the diner. "Goodbye, Damon."

"Impossible."

Kit looked over her shoulder at the gruff recognition in Damon's voice. "Damon? Get on the damn ladder and climb with me."

His expression was focused on some other

place, at some other time. He wasn't with her. "I know that voice."

"Damon!"

There was no time to ask him whom it belonged to.

Another strand on the cable snapped above them and spiraled down through the air toward them.

The elevator was going to crash.

And it would take the man she loved with it.

Chapter Twelve

"Damon!"

The man was frozen. The elevator was shaking.

What was it in his face that tortured him so? The sound of a friend's voice? A betrayal too heinous for a man who rarely gave his trust?

She'd give him another voice to listen to. "Damon!"

A third strand of the cable snapped, and the elevator canted at a dangerous angle. He stumbled to his knees and slid toward the edge. "Damon!"

Kit hurried back down, but her voice had been enough. Damon lifted his chin, glared her back from stepping off the ladder, and scrambled to his feet. "Go, sweetheart." He grabbed the backs of her thighs and pushed her upward. "Climb."

"You stay with me," she warned, frightened that he'd slip away from her again.

"I'm right behind you."

The unnatural stress must have popped a brake

loose from its track because the elevator dropped again. Three more inches. Damon reached for the ladder. Another strand snapped. A brake popped. Two inches more.

Kit climbed. Damon shifted his weight onto the ladder. One of the bolts scraped from its mooring and shot out. It hit the far wall, then pinged and rolled and fell away into nothingness.

"Go!" Damon shouted. The bolts struggled to grip the crumbling concrete. Kit reached the steel ledge above the faded *16* painted onto the concrete-block wall. "Careful," Damon warned.

She was at the far end from the gate's hasp. Kit stepped onto the few inches of ledge. She curled her fingers through the gate's cross bars and tiptoed across.

Beneath her, the elevator shook as it fought to hold its grip. Above her a strand of steel cable cut through the air. "Look out!"

She clung to the gate and Damon hugged the wall as the cable whipped past them and crashed onto the top of the elevator. Chunks of concrete pulverized. Sparks flew. A third brake popped off its track and the car jerked and righted itself. It began to shimmy downward. The fourth brake couldn't hold.

The cable was splintering above them, filling the shaft with deadly reverberations like gunfire.

"Kit!"

Damon had reached the top of the ladder.

She closed her fingers around the lock.

The last brake surrendered. The cable exploded with a final snap.

"Katherine!"

The world opened up beneath her feet as the elevator plummeted into the darkness.

Kit pushed the gate open, fell onto the floor and crawled back to the ledge to reach for Damon.

The elevator hit bottom with the force of two semis ramming head-on at high speed. A deafening roar rushed up the shaft. Damon grabbed the ledge. The stench of decades-old dust was pushed ahead of the debris flying toward them.

"Damon!" Kit grabbed a handful of sweater and pulled for all she was worth to help Damon haul himself up over the ledge.

The smack of wind hit her face an instant before Damon whipped his arms around her. He rolled her beneath him just as the explosive shock wave blew out into every open floor it passed. Shreds of concrete and steel and age-old dirt pelted Damon's back like a hail storm.

Kit buried her face in his chest and held on until the dust had settled.

When it was quiet again, Kit tried to wedge some space between them. A coating of gray dust had turned his black sweater to charcoal. She wanted to see his face, touch him. "Are you all right?"

But he'd had the same thought. His hands were hard and urgent on her as he inspected her from head to toe. "Are you hurt?"

"I'm fine." Even his eyepatch was a dusty gray. She brushed her fingertips across his jaw, verifying that his fierce expression meant he was fighting mad, not fighting pain. "I'm scared. Confused. But fi—"

He brushed aside the dust that had fallen onto her lips and replaced his thumb with his mouth. Damon's kiss was hard and potent and over before she could even catch her breath.

Then she was sneezing and he was smiling. He rolled off her, rolled to his feet and held out a hand to help her stand. "Thank you." He dipped his mouth and kissed her again. A quick peck on the lips. A stamp of possession. "Do you have sixteen flights of stairs in you?"

Kit nodded. "I sure don't have another elevator ride in me."

Without ever releasing her hand, Damon jogged to the opposite end of the hallway and led her onto the stairs. "We'll see what damage has been done first. I'll get a key card from Kronemeyer, right before I fire his ass. Then we can take the penthouse elevator to find out what the hell happened upstairs."

"I want to check on Matt and Germane."

It took them seven minutes to reach the lobby. Another ten to make sure that no one on the ground floor was injured. While Germane called the police and fire departments, Kit and Damon climbed into the rubble pit at the base of the elevator shaft.

The car itself had imploded, folding in on itself like a crushed soda can. But the impact had shattered concrete walls and blown out parts of the support structure at the base of the shaft, leaving pockets of empty space large enough to stand up in.

She was in one of those air pockets when she screamed. Damon was at her side in an instant, hugging her against his chest and turning her away from the gruesome site of Henry Phipps's mangled body. Kit wrapped her arms around his waist and clutched handfuls of his sweater. She hadn't seen *dead* before. Only in forensic labs and funeral parlors, but never like this. "Do you think Henry fell down the shaft? Or did someone push him? Do you think he suffered?"

Had he snuck back upstairs to find an apartment to borrow for the night, and run across something—or someone—he shouldn't?

"Looks like his neck is broken to me. But I can't tell if it was accidental or intentional. Or even if it came from a fall." Damon smoothed her hair, stroked her back. Then he suddenly stopped and growled into her ear. "It never ends."

"What?"

"No, don't look." But she had already turned to see the skeleton of the decomposing body that had been dislodged from the walls by the crash. An unnamed corpse didn't bother her so much as an old friend whom she'd miss.

Ignoring Damon's protests, Kit climbed over the rubble to inspect the body. "This guy's been here a year. Maybe a little longer."

The crumbling grout and debris crunched beneath Damon's boots and he walked over and knelt beside her. "Did he fall down the shaft, too?"

"Not unless the bullet knocked him off a ledge." She pointed to the neat hole at the center of his skull.

"The curse of Sinclair's Folly. No wonder Kronemeyer can't keep a full crew working here."

"What's that on your boot?" Kit reached over and scraped a fingertipful of fine powder from where the suede was stitched to his crepe sole.

"I picked that up by Henry's body. There's concrete and plaster dust all over the floor."

Kit rolled the dust between her thumb and fingers. "But it's pink. Not as gritty." She carried it to her nose and sniffed. Curious. "It's sweet." Fruity.

Like a crushed antacid tablet.

Kit's stomach dropped as quickly as the elevator had fallen. "Where *is* Kronemeyer?"

But Damon didn't answer. He was on his feet again, staring up into the darkness above them.

Kit stood beside him. "Oh, my God."

She heard it, too. An eerily familiar sound, one that Kit's parents would have been able to hear—to testify to—one dark night eighteen months ago.

All the way from the top of the elevator shaft.

Fire.

KIT'S PARENTS had been murdered. Because of him. Damon had no doubts about the logic of that explanation. Two men lay dead at the bottom of the elevator shaft. Because of him.

He and Kit were supposed to be down there, too. His fault, again.

It had taken the resolute determination of every cell in his body to leave her behind, beyond his protective sight, while he rode up the penthouse elevator to see if his fiery nightmare was reliving itself on the twenty-ninth floor. But someone needed to be there to direct the firefighters when they arrived and to give a statement to the police.

If he hadn't reminded her that Matt could be in danger, too, and needed someone to watch over him, Damon suspected she'd be searching for a way to come after him, a way to help, a way to stick her beautiful, freckled nose into his business and save his sorry ass.

God, that woman had fight in her. She'd never give up on anything, or anyone. Not even him.

Unlike Miranda, who'd given up on their marriage, given up on life.

Who'd made him think he had to give up on life, too.

But Katherine Elizabeth Snow made him want to live, want to fight, want to love. He *did* love. Her.

He didn't deserve her. And if he never had a chance to make things right with her—either because of what waited for him on the twenty-ninth floor or his own stubborn ignorance when it came to interacting with people—at least he had last night with her. At least he knew she'd be safe.

The elevator passed the twenty-seventh floor. The sad trick of it was that the key cards were just a shortcut. Anyone could use the penthouse elevator if they knew the entire coded sequence. He'd told Kit, just in case the firefighters or police needed to investigate something upstairs. Needed to retrieve another body that couldn't wait for all those stairs.

She'd been incredulous at how simple the code was. More incredulous that his equations were equally easy to decipher. It was all smoke and mirrors. The simplicity of his security system had stumped would-be hackers and industrial spies for years. They expected something brilliantly complicated from a man like him.

But what did it matter now?

The people who had destroyed his lab eighteen months ago were back with a vengeance. They'd set up shop on one of the tower's empty floors—to tap into the penthouse lab's electrical conduits and computer relays. To be close enough to commit the sabotage that would keep construction workers away. To give them easy access to the penthouse levels without using the elevators. To give them dozens of places to hide, right under his nose.

Kit remembered the boxes in Henry Phipps's adopted apartment. Hastily removed as though never there. But Henry must have discovered them. What had he found? Computer equipment? Explosives? Bottles of Formula 428 and other bastardized potions from his stolen work?

The missing, injured—dead—construction workers must have all seen or heard something they shouldn't. And a bastard who would kill a defenseless seventy-nine-year-old woman wouldn't hesitate to kill anyone else who stood in his way.

When the elevator slowed and bounced to a

stop, Damon squeezed his fists at his sides, trying to equalize the tension and dread warring inside him. He'd already theorized what to expect when those doors opened.

But scientific theory couldn't prepare him for reality.

The heat hit him first. He raised his hand and shielded his eye. The door to his lab had been blown open. A cabinet inside was burning, along with a stack of books and papers. The fire was licking its way up the wall toward the ceiling.

Then he saw the tall, blond woman with a gun—and Damon died inside all over again.

Miranda.

He braced his hand against the door to keep it open, unsure for a moment whether or not he'd re-entered his nightmare. But this was real. The gun she held with a handkerchief wrapped around the butt was real. The fire was real.

Miranda Sinclair was real.

The skin on her face had regrown with the same plastic texture of his hands. She'd undergone some cosmetic surgery that didn't completely mask the scar lines along her jaw and temples. The long blond hair was fake, but the blue eyes were the same as the ones he'd last seen in the asylum. Cold. Conscienceless. Full of blame and hate.

"I hoped I was hallucinating when I heard your voice."

"Hello, darling."

"You continued with the regeneration therapy. Even though you know it's toxic to your system."

"Yes, one of these days we'll have to talk about how you failed me." She smiled. It was cold and fake and lacked the compassion he'd seen shining in dozens of Kit's smiles.

Damon felt nothing inside but guilt and regret. "I see you disabled the sprinkler system. Again."

"Not me, darling. I hired a brute who could do more than just bed me on the weekends."

"Kronemeyer?"

"Bravo. You figured it out. Nearly two years after the fact. All brains and not a lick of sense when it comes to dealing with people. Just like always. It's a wonder SinPharm has survived without me." She motioned him out of the elevator with a sharp movement of the gun. "Now come inside. I need you to do something for me. And this time you're going to get it right."

The gun barrel pressed to Damon's skull hardly bothered him anymore. The flames creeping closer to the *K26* experiment—Kit's Formula now, no longer Miranda's—did.

"I'm telling you, that's the code."

Miranda seemed incensed that the numbers could be that simple. "My birth date? In a rotating sequence?"

She hadn't figured it out. Her dead hacker

hadn't figured it out. But Damon hadn't hesitated to tell her. He wanted her out of the growing fire, away from the melting walls and burning pockets of chemicals. He didn't want any more deaths— even hers for a second time—on his conscience.

He pulled up the regeneration formula on his computer screen and stood, defying the press of the gun. "There's your damn formula. Unfiltered. No codes. Take it. Sell it for millions. Let's just get out of here."

"I have *this* face because of some sentimental crap you came up with?"

Her chest rose and fell in shallow, quick breaths. But the wheezing told him it was the fumes gathering in the air, not the stress, that was getting to her. He reached for her arm. "C'mon. The smoke's starting to affect your breathing."

"Get your ugly hands off me!" She shook him off and jabbed the gun into his stomach to hold him at bay while she typed in an e-mail address. "Send it all to this mailbox."

"Fine." She shifted the gun to his kidney as he bent over the keyboard and sent the equations. He swiped the sweat from his face as he stood. "Done. Now we leave. Your lungs are already damaged. We need to get out of here."

"Not *we,* darling. Me." She stroked her long fingernails across his cheek. When Damon flinched at the repulsive imitation of a caress, she ground the gun into his waist, looped her hand behind his neck and forced his head down for a kiss. Damon spat her taste from his mouth as she laughed. "Now be a good boy and die."

She raised the gun to his empty eye.

"Damon?"

Son of a bitch.

Kit's hopeful voice reached deep into his heart and squeezed it in a fist when J. T. Kronemeyer dragged her into the lab at gunpoint. The bastard had his hands on her. The angle of his gun could pierce a lung or stop her valiant heart.

But she was the one who apologized. "I'm sorry, Doc. I told him the elevator code. He was going to shoot Matt."

"You did the right thing, sweetheart. It's okay."

"Sweetheart?" Miranda's mocking laugh came out as little more than a wheeze. She pressed her palm to her temple as she turned around. "Dear Kit, you give me such a headache." But she unleashed her anger at Kronemeyer. "I told you to get rid of her."

The black-haired brute fought right back. "Hey, you had two chances to kill her and screwed it up. At the hospital and at that café. So now we're gonna try it my way. It'll look like an accident if she dies in the fire."

"You two are way beyond making anything look like an accident." Kit only fueled the tension.

"Shut up!" The contractor jerked her arm, and Kit yelped.

"Kronemeyer!" Damon's warning was met with a gun in his face.

But Miranda's wrath was all for her lover. "I don't pay you to think, J.T. I pay you to do. Exactly as I say."

"Maybe that's why I haven't seen any of my money yet. I intend to speed the process to get those millions you promised me."

With the fire behind him hot enough to singe the skin on his back, two guns, greed and maniacs surrounding him, Damon realized reasoning wouldn't work to get them out of there. But bargaining might.

"I found a tissue regeneration formula that works with your chromosomal makeup. It's in the preliminary stages, but it works. I don't know if it can repair the brain damage that's been done, or affect the hormonal levels in your system—"

"Brain damage? Hormones?"

Damon didn't back away from the gun or Miranda. "It can't give you your personality or your heart back. It can't make you give a damn about anyone besides yourself. But it could give you back your face. It could make you physically beautiful again if that's what you want."

"What I want…is the money that I earned for you. For your company. What I want is what's rightfully mine. Instead of giving away your fortune to hapless charities, pouring it into dying neighborhoods—thinking of nothing but research when we could have been rich—"

"We were rich. We had each other. We had a future."

"Your future. Not mine. They were your millions, Damon. SinPharm's millions. We were supposed to be equal partners. Where were my millions?"

A section of the ceiling crashed to the floor behind him, and Damon jumped. Miranda retreated a step.

Kit interrupted. "Could we have this discussion somewhere else?"

"Miranda," Kronemeyer prompted.

But the wildness in Miranda's eyes made Damon think that the fire scared her as much as it scared him. It was the first glimpse of humanity he'd seen in her. She seemed confused, lost, as the emotion crept in.

Seeing her as a lost cause, Kronemeyer turned his attention back to Damon. "You've got a formula that works?"

"Yes. Right here in the lab." He nodded toward Kit. "Let her go and I'll get it for you."

"Get it first, and then I'll think about letting her go."

Damon glanced over his shoulder toward the

exit leading up to the penthouse. There'd be no escape that direction. The smoke that had been gathering above the ceiling panels rolled in, eating up the oxygen in the room. The fire was cutting an unforgiving path straight for them. And he was about to lose his bargaining chip.

"Fine."

"Be careful." Kit's words strengthened him, sharpened his senses and tore away any last concerns about what he had to do.

He crouched beneath the smoke and crossed to the row of microscopes. The fire was already heating the metal table. Damon used the hem of his sweater as a hot pad to retrieve the *K26* petri dish.

"Here." Miranda was coughing now, a shallow, wretched sound. Damon moved past her and extended his arm and the *K26* to Kronemeyer. "Now let her go."

"I don't think so, Doc."

In the split second it took Kronemeyer to tuck the plastic dish into his shirt pocket, Damon charged, twisting his body between Kit and the gun.

"Damon!"

Kit went flying and Damon and Kronemeyer crashed to the floor. This was the monster who'd taken a lead pipe to Helen's skull. He damn well was going to duke it out with someone his own size this time.

The two men rolled and punched. They hit a table leg, and dozens of beakers and vials shattered on the floor around them. Kronemeyer's fist connected with Damon's jaw. Damon knocked the gun from his hand. The contractor clawed at Damon's eye and came away with nothing but eyepatch. Damon shoved the man off him and lunged at his throat.

But there was no fighting left to be done. One of the glass shards had severed the artery in Kronemeyer's neck. The man was bleeding out. Even if Damon wanted to, it was too late to save him. Kronemeyer's terrified eyes glazed open and still.

"Maybe you'll clean up the mess you make next time."

Winded from the fight, and finding little oxygen in the air to revive his strength, Damon was slow to react to the ominous click of a bullet sliding into its firing chamber. He knew it wasn't pointed at him. But he'd have given every penny in his bank account to have it that way as he slowly stood and turned to see Miranda, coughing blood into her handkerchief now, but keeping a steady enough hand to aim the bullet at Kit's temple.

He raised his hands in surrender.

But she wasn't interested in negotiating. "What'll it be, Damon? A bullet through her brain like the sap I hired to steal your formulas in the first place? Or should I let her die by your hand?" She pocketed the handkerchief and pulled out a syringe. He had no doubt it was loaded with the deadly 428 serum.

He looked hard at Kit, focused every ugly inch of his expression on her, willing her to understand that he would die before he'd allow that woman to hurt her any more.

Those pale-gray eyes were just as intense. And that bravery frightened him more than the gun or the syringe.

"That would be poetic justice, wouldn't it?" Miranda was oblivious to the silent exchange. "A rich man, devoting all his time to saving lives. Your work will kill her, and I'll have your money. Fitting, I think."

Damon shifted his attention to the shell of the woman he'd once loved. "Did I do this to you?"

"Do not blame yourself for this wacko, Damon. Look how she's hurt you, used you, betrayed you. All you did was try to help her. You nearly lost your life trying to save hers. I've seen you dead inside with grief for her."

Damon shook his head. "I don't feel that grief anymore. My wife is long gone. The woman I once loved couldn't have killed your parents or Old Henry. Or Helen. I don't know this woman. But I swear to God, if she hurts you—I'll kill her myself."

"Oh, save the soap opera." Miranda raised the syringe.

"Save yourself, bitch." Kit rammed her fist under Miranda's arm, knocking it over her head and sending the liquid death flying through the air.

"Kit!"

The syringe hit the floor and shattered. The serum caught fire. The toxic fumes it would release would be poison to both women.

Damon lunged toward them. "Get out of here!"

But Kit whirled around with a roundhouse punch and knocked Miranda back into the flames. Her screams were instant. Strident.

And Kit's momentum carried her into the flames right behind her.

"Kit!" A wall of roiling smoke shot up between them, and Damon couldn't see her, couldn't reach her. "Kit!"

"Damon!" That was Miranda's voice, her wrenching cough. "Help me!"

He hesitated a moment, staring his nightmare right in the face.

"Damon!" Miranda was dying. "Help me!"

Then he heard Kit's voice. "Go! Go, Damon. Save yourself. You deserve to live!"

"Damon!"

"Take care of Matt for me. And Germane. Take care of yourself." She was coughing now. "But go. Just go!"

Damon Sinclair had plunged into the flames once before to save the woman he loved.

He'd do it again.

Chapter Thirteen

"Kit?" Matt stuck his head through the kitchen door, and she looked up from the vat of coleslaw she was mixing. "You'd better come out here."

"What now?" She covered the slaw with plastic wrap, wiped her hands on a towel and followed her brother into the diner.

Two weeks had passed since her release from the hospital for treatment of minor burns and smoke inhalation, and other than his late-night visits to the hospital to sit with her while she slept, Damon hadn't made an appearance. He'd carried her from the fire, dragged Miranda out, too. He'd showered Kit with kisses, promised to make everything right, then had disappeared from her life.

She'd heard from Easting Davitz that Damon was spending some time getting Miranda settled in a new psychiatric hospital. She'd be held there until her trial, though her lawyers planned to plead insanity. She'd be spending whatever was left of her life in a prison for the criminally insane. Ken Kenichi had gone back to Japan with his son's body. The building and arson inspectors had certified that the first floor was safe for business and living. All but the lab itself—and the smoke-damaged penthouse above it—had passed inspection. So long as one didn't mind taking the stairs. The elevators were off-limits until every inch of the shafts, cables and cars had been screened for Kronemeyer's sabotage.

The snow was melting. Business had picked up at the diner. And Matt had shown up for work every day, and come home every night like clockwork.

Kit should be feeling better than this.

Missing Damon made her moody. But she was a champion at coping, at sucking it up and diving into her work feeding the new construction crew that Easting Davitz had hired.

Damon had saved her life, saved Matt, helped her and the police find answers to the mysteries surrounding the fires and thefts and murders at the Sinclair Tower—and he'd taught her how to love with her whole heart.

She believed, deep down, that he loved her, too.

But maybe it was asking too much for him to come down out of his lofty world and live in the reality that was hers.

The reality of a busy diner and a missing brother. "Matt?"

He popped up from a booth on the far side of the restaurant. "There's someone here who wants to meet you."

Curious.

But when Matt stepped aside, Kit's perplexed frown turned into a smile. "Helen."

Kit hurried across the diner as Matt helped the petite, white-haired woman to her feet. A stylish red hat covered the stitches on her head, and her small, fragile fingers reached out to greet Kit with the strength of a healthy woman. "Kit, dear."

"It's so good to see you. How are you feeling?" She wrapped the older woman up in a gentle hug, then sat down across the table from her.

Helen pushed her tea aside to reach for Kit's hand. "I'm fine, dear. I've been talking to that brother of yours. He needs to comb his hair, but he's quite charming. I asked him to send me his address when he goes to school in the fall."

"Oh?" Helen was adopting Matt? Matt was adopting her? This neighborhood truly was becoming the family Kit had envisioned it could be.

"Germane may know how to barbecue, but I bet I can bake a better cookie."

"Oatmeal chocolate-chip?"

"If that's what he wants. Damon always loved when I sent him care packages. I'd like to think my cooking was one of the things that made him so smart."

Kit adored this woman. "He loves you, period."

"I know. But let's talk about you, dear. You had some questions for me?"

"I did?"

"In the hospital. And I do hope we can continue reading those books. Maybe we could meet for tea and discuss them."

"I'd like that."

Helen smiled, then crooked a finger and asked Kit to lean in. The older woman whispered, "He has one on his behind."

He? One what?

"You'll have to see it in the light. It's a hydrogen molecule—one proton, one electron. Evenly balanced and always together." Oh, my God. Was this woman talking about a tattoo? "He did go through a rebellious phase. Nothing got pierced, though. I think it fits you two better than he ever imagined." Helen patted Kit's hand, her pale blue eyes deeply sincere. "And if you'll be patient with my boy, I think you'll find that he loves you very much."

"He does." The gruff voice caressed her ears from the booth behind her. "I do."

Kit's heart hammered in her chest as she slid from the booth and stood to meet him. "Damon."

He was here. In public. In daylight.

Towering over her in the same black sweater and jeans. Same eyepatch. Same broad shoulders and rugged face.

Different expression shining from his eye.

"I hear you've got good barbecue here."

Kit would have thrown herself into his arms and kissed him right there on the spot, but she suspected there were enough curious glances aimed their way. And he'd already taken a risk by coming here during the noontime rush. She'd give him his space so he wouldn't disappear into a shadow somewhere.

"The best in K.C."

"I've got a bet with Germane that I can figure out the ingredients in his sauce. It's strictly a matter of reducing it down to its chemical components."

Kit couldn't contain her smile. "Good luck with that one." Or her tears. "Why are you here?"

"Ah, don't do that, sweetheart." He reached out and caught a teardrop with the tip of his finger and brushed it from her cheek. "That's almost tougher than watching you lie in the hospital, fighting for your life."

"I'm tough."

Now he smiled. "Don't I know it."

"Can I get you something to eat?"

He gestured to the table where he'd been sitting. "Well, I wouldn't mind coming down from the penthouse to share lunch with a good neighbor. If that's what you want." Kit held her breath. She wanted that, yes, but so much more. "But I think there are some discussions that are still best done in private."

Kit thumbed over her shoulder. "The kitchen's empty right now."

"The kitchen it is."

"I'm proud of you for coming out to the diner like a regular—"

As soon as the door shut behind them, Damon turned her into his arms and kissed her. Kit looped her arms around his neck and held on, hungry for his touch, aching for his heat.

Several minutes passed before they came up for air. Kit was sitting on the kitchen counter. Damon stood between her legs, his hands on her hips, their foreheads touching as they breathed deeply to regain their composure.

"I love you, Katherine Snow." The gruff confession skittered along every nerve and suffused her with warmth.

"I love you, Dr. Sinclair."

The scrunchie that had held her ponytail in place had vanished and he was stroking his fingers through her hair. "You've healed me more than any doctor or formula I can devise could. You forced me to live. To be part of the world again. To be human."

"Oh, Damon." She cupped his face in her hands.

"No, let me get through this." He pulled her hands from his face and stepped back, letting her read the blend of need and uncertainty on his face. "My hands are never going to look any better than this. My face isn't gonna get handsome. I can work on the moods. But I want to ask you...I need to ask you...are you sure what you feel for me isn't morbid fascination? Or gratitude? Or even just lust?"

Kit tipped her head, considering that poignant admission of humanity in his words. "I love you, Damon. The scars and synthetic skin don't matter. I love the man you are inside—the man you are in spite of, or maybe because of, your scars."

He studied the sincerity in her eyes. Then his mouth curved with a wry laugh. "Ironic. That's what I told Miranda after the first fire. When there was still a hint of the woman I once loved inside her."

She waited a telling moment. "Okay, Dr. Logic. Did you believe it? When you said those words to Miranda, did you mean them?"

He did. The light went on. The smile reappeared. "Yes."

She reached for him then. "I love you. Believe *that*."

"What do you want, Kit? Anything, it's yours. Just name it."

"I want you."

"Done." He closed the distance between them, folded her into his arms and kissed her until they were both shaking with need. When he pulled away, his rusty voice held a mischief she'd never heard before. A boyish self-assurance she loved. "Now ask for something else."

"Will you continue mentoring Matt? He really seems to like and respect you."

"Absolutely. I want to. Now ask for something tough."

She thought a moment. Felt a little mischievous herself. She dropped her voice to a seductive whisper. "Show me your tattoo."

"Who told you I had a tat..." Damon shook his head and spun away, heading for the kitchen door. "Helen!"

Kit jumped down from the counter and hurried after him. She caught his hand and laughed. He held her tight—trading strengths, trading hope, trading love—and walked with her, together, into the diner.

* * * * *

Watch out for Julie Miller's new miniseries
THE PRECINCT: VICE SQUAD
this summer from Harlequin Intrigue.

UP AGAINST THE WALL—June 2007

NINE-MONTH PROTECTOR—July 2007

Happily ever after is just the beginning...

Turn the page for a sneak preview of
DANCING ON SUNDAY AFTERNOONS
by
Linda Cardillo

Harlequin Everlasting—Every great love
has a story to tell.™
A brand-new line from Harlequin Books
launching this February!

Prologue

Giulia D'Orazio
1983

I had two husbands—Paolo and Salvatore.

Salvatore and I were married for thirty-two years. I still live in the house he bought for us; I still sleep in our bed. All around me are the signs of our life together. My bedroom window looks out over the garden he planted. In the middle of the city, he coaxed tomatoes, peppers, zucchini—even grapes for his wine—out of the ground. On weekends, he used to drive up to his cousin's farm in Waterbury and bring back manure. In the winter, he wrapped the peach tree and the fig tree with rags and black rubber hoses against the cold, his massive, coarse hands gentling those trees as if they were his fragile-skinned babies. My neighbor, Dominic Grazza, does that for me now. My boys have no time for the garden.

In the front of the house, Salvatore planted roses. The roses I take care of myself. They are giant, cream-colored, fragrant. In the afternoons, I like to sit out on the porch with my coffee, protected from the eyes of the neighborhood by that curtain of flowers.

Salvatore died in this house thirty-five years ago. In the last months, he lay on the sofa in the parlor so he could be in the middle of everything. Except for the two oldest boys, all the children were still at home and we ate together every evening. Salvatore could see the dining room table from the sofa, and he could hear everything that was said. "I'm not dead, yet," he told me. "I want to know what's going on."

When my first grandchild, Cara, was born, we brought her to him, and he held her on his chest, stroking her tiny head. Sometimes they fell asleep together.

Over on the radiator cover in the corner of the parlor is the portrait Salvatore and I had taken on our twenty-fifth anniversary. This brooch I'm wearing today, with the diamonds—I'm wearing it in the photograph also—Salvatore gave it to me that day. Upstairs on my dresser is a jewelry box filled with necklaces and bracelets and earrings. All from Salvatore.

I am surrounded by the things Salvatore gave me, or did for me. But, God forgive me, as I lie alone now in my bed, it is Paolo I remember.

Paolo left me nothing. Nothing, that is, that my family, especially my sisters, thought had any value. No house. No diamonds. Not even a photograph.

But after he was gone, and I could catch my breath from the pain, I knew that I still had something. In the middle of the night, I sat alone and held them in my hands, reading the words over and over until I heard his voice in my head. I had Paolo's letters.

* * * * *

Be sure to look for
DANCING ON SUNDAY AFTERNOONS
available January 30, 2007.
And look, too, for our other
Everlasting title available,
FALL FROM GRACE by Kristi Gold.

FALL FROM GRACE is a deeply emotional story
of what a long-term love really means.
As Jack and Anne Morgan discover,
marriage vows can be broken—
but they can be mended, too.
And the memories of their marriage have
an unexpected power
to bring back a love that never really left....

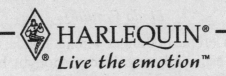